SUNSPACER

Bernal One

SUNSPACER

A NOVEL

George Zebrowski

HARPER & ROW, PUBLISHERS

Library of Congress Cataloging in Publication Data
Zebrowski, George, 1945–
    Sunspacer.

    Summary: Joe Sorby, a high school student of a future
century, has a longing for faraway places that eventually
takes him to a life of hardship and danger on the
planet Mercury and in the Rings of Saturn.
    [1. Science fiction.   2. Space colonies—Fiction]
I. Title.
PZ7.Z3Su 1984   [Fic]   79-2670
ISBN 0-06-026850-6 (lib. bdg.)
ISBN 0-06-026849-2 (pbk.)

CONTENTS

Books by George Zebrowski

Macrolife
The Monadic Universe
The Omega Point Trilogy
Sunspacer

Anthologies edited by George Zebrowski

Tomorrow Today
Human-Machines (with Thomas N. Scortia)
Faster Than Light (with Jack Dann)
Creations (with Isaac Asimov and Martin H.
  Greenberg)
Best of Thomas N. Scortia

For Joanne Ryder,
who encouraged this book,
held her breath,
and lived to see it.

And for Antonia Markiet,
who did the hard editing
and encouraging.

1 GETTING READY

Jupiter ballooned into view on the south wall of the cafeteria. The voyaging eye of the three-dee motion mural sailed by the giant planet, rotated gracefully to peer at a few major moons, then fixed its gaze on the long way to Saturn.

Chico Fernandez's tour loop of sunspace made the basement level of Bronx Science/DeWitt Clinton Commons into something like the brightly lit observation deck of a giant spaceship, but no one paid much attention. After you've rushed out from Mercury to Pluto a few times, the endless round trip begins to bore most people, despite the whip turns, long looks, and sudden speedups near the planets.

I looked at my empty bubble of nonfat milk, wondering if I wanted another, maybe with apple pie. There wouldn't be much time for me to talk to Morey Green-Wolfe before our two-o'clock physics class. He was late, as usual, and I felt irritated.

Home screens had been scrambled from May 15 to June 17, so classes would meet in person. High school students were usually brought together in January, May, and June, but graduating seniors could get away with only a month of staying together. Screen attendance made people shy, some educators claimed, but I had my doubts. It was true that there were sponges who liked to stay home and plunder the world's libraries at their own dizzy pace, but I knew of too many people who had met over the screen hooks to believe that becoming friends in that way was all that hard to do, or very harmful. Some people preferred to start out over the net. They would meet sooner or later, or not at all, but the system made it easier for shy people to get to know each other in the first place, without much chance of things going wrong. It was more like having an old-fashioned pen pal, except that the notes and letters were sent differently and more quickly. Still, I guess some of the hard cases among shy people needed to be thrown together. I knew there were adults who owned three-dee holos and who rarely met in the flesh. But those people were usually up to a century old or more, and wanted to cultivate their privacy. They had lived into our time from the last century, and their bodies had been renewed at least twice through organ clones and cell regeneration, so they were a special case.

I stood up from my seat at the end of the long table

and spotted Morey's broad shoulders near the north exit. He pushed through the outgoing crowd and came across the room, adjusting his collarless tweed jacket and brushing back his dark brown hair.

"Sorry, Joe," he said loudly as he slipped in across from me and shook his head. "Old Lyons and super-gravity. He doesn't seem to know—" He gave me a blank look as I sat down. "What's wrong?"

"You're late and I wanted to talk."

He glanced at the wall timer. "Sorry. You have your acceptance letter?" He bit his lower lip. "Look, I said I'm going. It's all set. Your parents still edgy about it? You *know* they can't stop you." He was looking right at me. "What is it—you don't want me for a roommate?"

"It's not that. I've been wondering."

He examined me with his steel-blue eyes. I looked down at the table, feeling foolish. "I guess I'm worried about going off-planet to college."

He sighed. "It's the best school we could get into, one of the best anywhere."

"It's the idea of actually going away from everything, outside the atmosphere . . ."

"Nothing to worry about." He seemed a bit surprised. "You know what it's like out there. Space won't bite you."

"Knowing is one thing, feeling another."

He shook his head. "No. You're spooking yourself. You're just apprehensive about leaving home."

"Maybe that's it." I felt silly, especially after all the convincing I had gone through with my parents. A part of me was uneasy while the rest of me was looking forward to the change. It was hard to admit that I wanted to get away from my parents. "We're late," I said.

"Forget it—we've got the grades." He looked around. "I'll be glad to leave this place."

"It's not so bad," I said feebly.

A tray crashed to the floor. Morey gave me a bored look as the cheers started. "Screening is better than this."

"You've got to keep up your social development."

"With this herd? I'd probably go into shock if they didn't cheer!"

I knew how he felt, but the noise had calmed me down. As I looked around at the faces, I realized that most of the students didn't seem to demand much from themselves. They were looking forward to the moment when they could freeze their educations and be ready for job slots with guaranteed vacations. I said I wanted a scientific career, but Morey seemed to want one more than I did. Sure, I liked physics and astronomy, but I could probably live without making some giant discovery. Morey wanted to explain the whole universe.

"What else is there worth trying for?" he liked to ask. "We know a lot, but it's still a mystery." I felt like an outcast for not quite being able to see what he meant.

"Feeling better?" he asked.

4

"Yeah, I guess."

Morey laughed. "Old Lyons is five years behind in astrophysics, maybe ten." It might just as well have been a hundred, I thought.

"Might as well check our math presentation," I said, taking out my flatscreen and thumbing up the problems. The display insisted on presenting a flicker of random numbers, so I wiped it with a pass of my hand and looked up.

Marisa Granville was standing behind Morey with two of her friends. Willow was in my English class; Corazon was a new girl from Jamaica.

"So you're going," Marisa said, staring at me with her green eyes.

I nodded.

"Out there."

"Yeah."

Morey swung his chair around. "What's so unusual? People have been leaving the planet for almost a century."

Marisa took a deep breath. Corazon shrugged; Willow smiled. I squinted at Morey, to warn him off; the conversation was going to be about something else, and I didn't want him in it.

"You think you're better than the rest of us," Marisa said. "Earth isn't good enough for you."

Corazon frowned. Marisa had not come to say goodbye, as I had hoped. She was still angry about my leaving.

"You obviously think it's glamorous," Morey said. I tensed, wishing that he would shut up.

Marisa was looking at me as if Morey were invisible. "I don't really care," she said. Willow smiled nervously, reminding me of the times she'd acted as go-between when Marisa and I'd had fights.

"Don't you know *anything*?" Morey asked, and I felt sorry for Marisa. Morey's critical tone was enough to freeze the oxygen in the air on a summer day. He knew how to ask questions in a way that destroyed the possibility of any answer, much less a reply that would interest him.

"Spacers think they're special," Marisa shot back. "Why do you want to go among people who think we're only bugs crawling around on the outside of a mudball?"

I knew it was all just talk that she'd picked up, that she was trying to get around to something else, but Morey just wouldn't let go, so maybe he deserved it.

"The mud's in your head," he replied. "Earth can't do without the power and resources that the Sunspace colonies provide. Maybe you need a dose of memory fix."

He was right, of course. I thought of the miners on Mercury. They were having a tough time getting what they needed from Earth, even though they gave Earth all the metals it needed. But this was not the time to discuss Earth's political problems.

"Joe, can I talk to you alone?" Marisa asked. Willow led Corazon away.

Morey finally caught on. "Uh, I'm going to get something to drink." He got up and left. Marisa slipped into his seat.

"You're not like him," she said softly. "So why are you going?"

"I want to be a physicist. It's the best school for it."

She didn't seem to believe me. I had wanted her to tell me that we were still friends, even if we had to go our separate ways. But she seemed to think that I was making a big mistake of some kind. She had never liked anything I was interested in, and she still didn't like Morey.

"It's not *you*," she said.

"What does that mean?"

"You don't understand, do you?"

"So tell me. You're not very clear about it." All I could see was that she didn't want me to go.

"You're too wrapped up in yourself to listen."

She was making me angry. "Look, I can be what I want."

She gave me a hopeless look as she stood up. "Well, I hope you'll both be very happy out there." She turned and bumped into Morey, then walked away.

Morey sat down. "Thanks," I said. "You really helped."

"It's all in knowing how to read weak minds," he announced stiffly, as if he were a million years old.

"Marisa's mind isn't weak. She just wants different things, that's all." I was suddenly impatient to leave. One more week and it would all be over.

"Sorry," Morey said. "You should have seen the look I got. She still cares about you, I bet."

It wasn't fair of Marisa to stir me up again. I hadn't seen her in three months and thought it was all over, but I could see why she had done it. This had been her last chance to get me to see myself her way. I felt guilty and relieved at the same time. I didn't care; I couldn't care—I was leaving.

"She didn't have to put down Sunspacers," I said, remembering the recent news stories about how many miners had died over the years in the quakes on Mercury.

"Just a handy needle to stick you with," Morey said. "I doubt she knows much about the politics. Earth's dependence on off-planet power and industry is making a lot of politicos hysterical, and they pass the feeling on to the populace. They hate the idea that a new civilization is growing out there and Earth is no longer everything."

"She was talking about other stuff."

"I know, that's what I meant. Where is she going?"

"Hawaii, I think."

He shrugged. "It's not known for anything besides some history."

8

"I don't think she got in anywhere else."

"What's she going to do?"

"Art, I think. Who cares?"

"She's not too happy with herself, so she came over to pick on you."

"Yeah, I know." She still wanted me to be someone else, and for a moment she had made me feel that I didn't know myself at all. I didn't like the feeling.

"How are your parents?"

"They seem to be getting along." Morey was beginning to irritate me. "Time to go home." I stood up and clipped my flatscreen to my belt. "See you tomorrow." There was no way I would be able to concentrate on two-o'clock physics.

A plate clattered somewhere as I made for the exit, and the cheering started up again.

As it got closer to graduation, I began to suspect that Mom and Dad would not be back in time. They hadn't been home during the last week of school. Dad had taken a leave from his job at the Institute and followed Mom to Brasilia after their last fight, on the day their marriage contract had come up for renewal. This bothered me in ways I didn't want to examine, so I tried to push it away.

I went to the exam terminals for five days of tests and got my A's, but there was little fun in it, even when I got the scholarship. I would have had to get double A's, if there were such a thing, to impress my parents or advisors. I knew one thing, though—I had to work much harder than Morey.

On the night before graduation, I was eating dinner alone again. There had been no calls or messages. I didn't even know if invitations had gone out to relatives. The only good thing about it all was that it kept me from thinking too much about Marisa. Cruel as it may sound, I had wanted her to fade away in my mind, but her talk with me in the cafeteria had made getting over her harder.

I got up and walked over to the window in the living room. The lights of Manhattan were blurry in my eyes. Maybe my parents would be back late tonight, I thought as I began to pace. I stopped after a moment and looked at the empty chairs around the triangular table in the dining area. The old-fashioned three-bulb chandelier seemed to be hanging at an angle. I hadn't eaten much of the tuna and crisp bread I had prepared. The split of white wine was unopened.

I looked out the picture window again, and saw myself in the dark glass. Suddenly, I was surprised by the fact of being *me*. Dad had once told me that the sensation would fade as I grew up, but I still couldn't see how that could happen. I was separate from other people, locked up in my own skull, unable to enter their heads any more than they could invade mine. So how could Marisa know me better than I did? But maybe she knew enough;

after all, I knew Mom and Dad, and cared about them, even if I didn't know *everything*.

The person staring back at me from the night seemed thin for five eight. His muscular arms were pale in the sleeveless blue shirt. He stooped a bit, and some of his light-brown hair fell over his right eye. His lower half faded away into the city lights.

—Why should I bother going to graduation?

—You were looking forward to it.

—No big thing. College is more important.

—Morey will expect you.

—He doesn't need me to graduate.

—But he's your best friend.

Maybe that was the only reason I was going off-planet to school. That and to get away from my parents. I was sick of them not getting along. So I would have to work a bit harder than Morey—so what? I would see a new way of life, human beings building new worlds among the stars. If it meant studying physics for a career, then I would do so. I was looking forward to being on my own, to not having to worry about anyone else for a while. I needed a big change, and this was going to be it.

I stepped closer to the window, feeling a bit lost; the floating figure disappeared.

2 GRADUATION

I got up the next morning, put on the one-piece blue corduroy suit Dad had bought me for the ceremony, and rode the boost tube up to the Educational Center on 210 Street West. It was almost ten A.M. when I arrived on level two above the street and came out into a hot, sunny day.

I felt lost as I looked out over the emptiness of the giant square around the hundred-story pyramid. Its east face caught the sun with a million windows, giving the structure the appearance of a cheerful ornament, but I wasn't in any mood to appreciate it. Maybe Mom and Dad had shown up at the last minute and were waiting inside. I would have missed them if I hadn't come, I told myself.

I wandered down the ramp and marched across the deserted square, working up a sweat by the time I reached the main doors. They slid open and I went into the lobby, loosening the stick seal on my collar as I looked around at the crowd.

I turned and saw Morey with his parents.

"Good morning, Joe," Mrs. Green-Wolfe said. I noticed some familiar faces behind them, but everyone was so dressy I couldn't be sure.

I nodded absentmindedly to Morey's mother. She always seemed to be smiling as if she knew some silly secret.

"Where's your folks?" Mr. Green-Wolfe asked loudly. Nearly everything he said sounded as if he were asking you whether you wanted a dessert. It was obvious where Morey got some of his manner from, except that he was smarter than his father.

I continued scanning the crowd. "Oh . . . they're here somewhere, with some relatives, I think. They were coming back late from a trip," I added, preparing the excuse I might need later.

"Your dad's a sharp econometrist," Mr. Green-Wolfe said, looking around as if he expected to get some business advice from him. "Your mother is a charming woman," he added. "I'll be so glad to see her again." He put his arm around my shoulder. "Do you think you boys will be able to stand sharing one dorm room together?"

"Sure," I managed to say, realizing that my parents weren't here. My face was flushed and I felt cheated. Suddenly all their excuses from other times added up into one big pain. I took a slow deep breath and tried not to show it, but it hurt just the same.

13

"Good!" Mr. Green-Wolfe said. "You two are real pals."

The time came to go into the auditorium. Scholarship winners sat together near the front, so I just tagged along automatically after Morey, not paying much attention to anything as we took our seats. Parents sat in the balconies, like elder gods gazing down on their creations. Maybe Mom and Dad were up there, but I was afraid to turn around for even a quick look.

Holo cams cast three-dees of speakers and students above the stage during the ceremony. Havelock "Burning Bush" Bearney, our red-bearded principal, delivered a dull talk about brains and courage and leadership, though he seemed to want us to opt for cooperation if we couldn't be leaders. Toshiro Saada, the class president, whispered a speech about sacrifice that seemed to exalt self-punishment. Elene Chen, valedictorian and math prodigy, gave a vague but well-organized address on setting your mind toward the right individual goals. My mind wandered as our names were read out in reverse alphabetical order.

"Joseph Sorby!"

My name echoed through the auditorium. Morey nudged me when I failed to react.

I went up to get my diploma, sleepwalking all the way. A giant image of me gazed at the blue ceiling as I marched up and took the tube of silvery plastic from "Burning Bush" Bearney. He shook my hand and grinned at me

14

with threatening teeth. Strangers applauded for me as I went down on the other side. I imagined Marisa making fun of me from her seat among my nine hundred classmates. Morey clapped me on the shoulder as I sat down, and that made me feel good, but I was still anxious to get it over with.

We finally marched out into the lobby. The doors slid open as the picture taking and gift giving began, and the whole show pushed out into the glare of the noon sun. No one noticed as I slipped away toward the station.

The tubeway boosted me down to 125 Street in a few minutes. I changed for the local and floated over to West 87. Anything would have been better than going home just then; I was mad and getting madder by the second.

A cool breeze was blowing through Central Park when I came up to street level and started down the block to our housing complex. I came to our outside elevator doors and pressed my palm on the printlock. The doors slid open and I stepped inside, feeling apprehensive as the elevator climbed the side of the building. I would be angry if my parents were home, angrier if they weren't. The breeze rolled the tops of the trees in the park. Afternoon sunlight cast sharp shadows between the tall buildings. The elevator rushed to the ninetieth floor and the inner doors opened.

I hesitated, staring southward to the blue ocean beyond lower New York. Finally I turned away and went inside, wandering slowly down the brightly lit hallway to our apartment.

Queasiness flooded my stomach as I thumbed the lock plate. I didn't know what I was going to do or say if they were home.

Mom jumped me as the door slid open. "I'm so sorry, dearest!" I tried to step back, but it was too late. "We just got back." She hugged me.

"Missed a connection," Dad said.

"Sure," I mumbled. My arms hung at my sides.

"Congratulations," Dad said.

Mom was looking into my eyes. Her black hair was piled on her head in a strange swirl. Her face was pale, sad, without makeup, and her eyes were slightly red.

They had tried to get back, a part of me said, but I wanted to hurt them for making me feel like nothing, even though I could see that they had already been hurting each other.

"There are messages for you," Dad said as I pulled free of Mom and went past him into the living room.

"Thanks," I said coldly, suddenly grateful for something else to do. I sat down by the phone and pressed in my thumbprint.

The wall screen lit up with my first message:

Mr. Joseph Sorby:

> Please report July 1, 2056,
> Bernal Hall, Dorm Room 108,
> O'Neill College,
> Dandridge Cole University at L–5
>
> *—Office of the Dean of Students*
> June 21, 2056

The second message appeared:

> *Dearest Joe:* [flashing letters]
>
> Cheers for our favorite
> grandson! We called earlier.
> Here's something to help you
> on your way, right into your
> new account #000–112–234789.
> We'll call you when you're
> settled at school. Love,
>
> *—Antonia and John Sorby*
> *London, June 21, 2056*

"Can I see?" Dad asked. The message flashed three times and blinked off. "Oh—is there anything from your mother's parents?"

END OF MESSAGES

I ignored him. The screen went dark.

"There will be one along," Mom said, sitting down on the arm of my chair. "I told them."

"Don't," I said as she touched my shoulder.

"We love you very much," she said with difficulty, leaning back next to me and closing her eyes. I remembered playing with her when I was small, sitting on her belly and shouting for her to surrender. She still seemed as beautiful, but she wasn't the same person.

There was a long silence. Dad stood nervously in the center of the room, as if waiting for something.

"Your mother and I will be separating," he said finally. "Sorry to have to tell you now."

Mom sat up and looked at me. "We waited until you were ready for college."

"Why?" I demanded, feeling my anger rising again. "So it would be easier on you? Maybe you were planning to leave me a message about it?" It was obvious to me that they were still concerned solely with each other, and I was just another obstacle.

"You're older now," Mom said, ignoring what I had said. "You're ready to be on your own. The marriage contract happened to expire now. You can understand that."

I looked at Dad. He seemed lost. I wondered again why he had been so opposed to my going off-planet to school. Maybe he had thought that if I had gone to Columbia or NYU, it would have helped keep the marriage together.

"When you come home," Mom continued, jumping

past any consideration of my feelings, "you'll come here for part of the time, and to your grandparents in Brasilia, until I get a place of my own there. Eurico and Agata were very excited when I told them you would visit them."

"We'll always be here for you," Dad added tiredly.

Mom let out a deep breath, and I could tell that she was relieved. Dad wasn't about to start arguing again.

"When do you have to leave?" she asked me. Her lid was on tight, and nothing was going to blow it off.

"About ten days," I said, struggling to control myself.

Dad slumped down in the sofa. "How was the ceremony?" He was emotionally drained and physically exhausted from the trip. There was no fight left in him, and I saw my chance.

"Pretty boring. You didn't miss much." I tried to sound as sarcastic as possible by putting myself into Morey's million-year-old man mood, but it went right past them.

"We should have been there," Mom said sternly as she stood up. She looked thinner in her slacks. "We know and we're sorry. You don't have to excuse us." She sounded as if she were talking about some other people.

Dad was looking down at his feet. "Nothing can excuse it," he said as if he were speaking to Mom. I might just as well not have been in the room. "We'll make it up to you. . . ."

"Sure—how are you going to do that?" I demanded,

feeling crushed. "You don't listen to each other or to me. It was shitty of you not to make sure that you would be back in time. You could have done that! Do you hear me?"

Dad looked at me in surprise. *You don't need us anymore,* his eyes seemed to suggest, *so it doesn't matter what you say.* Well, maybe he wasn't thinking exactly that, but I was sure that he had no energy left to worry about me or my feelings. A small, distant part of me wondered if I had ever listened enough to understand their problems; but it was too late for me to care. In ten days I would be free.

"You probably didn't have any breakfast," Mom said.

"I'm not hungry."

"I'll make lunch," Dad said as he got to his feet. I sympathized with him for a moment. Why should he bother listening to me, or facing up to anything, when in two weeks we would all be apart?

Clouds covered the sun in the window, and we became shadows in the pale daylight. Mom followed Dad into the kitchenette. I watched them going through old, familiar motions, and remembered those times when I had felt warm and secure, knowing that little would change for a long time to come, and maybe never. Those bright, endless afternoons seemed far away now. An awful fear rushed through me. In a few years Mom and Dad would only be people who had once been parents. Would we like each other as adults? There was no way to know, so I tried hard not to care, and pushed the problem away.

Mom swore as she dropped something. I heard Dad take a deep breath. "Eva . . ." he started to say.

"Don't begin, John," she shot back. There was a long silence, as if they were standing perfectly still. "Joe!" Mom called to me. "We'll have lunch in here on the counter."

The sun came out and filled the room with light. I got up, realizing that not much would have been different even if they had come to graduation. I would still have wanted to get away. Their problems were not about to disappear overnight, and my being around wouldn't help much.

"Joe?" Mom called again.

"Coming," I managed to say. Maybe we all needed to lose each other for a while.

3 GOING

"Are you very sure?" Mom asked me.

"I'm sure," I answered without looking at her. It was almost time for me to go. I knew that they were relieved about my going, but it made them feel guilty, so they were repeating their old questions to make themselves feel better. I had gotten my way because they were too wrapped up in their problems to worry about me. If they had tried to force me to go to college while I lived at home, I would have complained against them under the Youth Rights Act of 2004.

"It's what he wants," Dad said as firmly as he could, more to settle Mom down than to support me. *And you'll be stuck with however it turns out.* He didn't say it out loud, but it was there in the tone of his voice.

We wandered toward the door. Mom held her hands together and tried to smile. "Are you sure the scholarship will cover everything?"

She knew it would, so why was she asking again? I

had to admit that it couldn't just be guilt. She cared about me, as much as she could, I realized.

"He's had expert help in the choice and planning," Dad said, standing there, hands deep in his loose pants.

Mom looked at him, then at me, unable to speak.

"Just a kid," Dad muttered. "Sitting on my arm only yesterday."

The lump in my throat surprised me as I picked up my small bag.

"All set with your trunk?" Dad asked in a quavering voice.

"Three days ago," I croaked. "You were here when they took it away."

He gave a strained laugh. "Right."

Mom sniffled, ready to cry.

"Well, good luck, son," Dad said loudly and held out his hand. It was no time to think or make judgments. I shook it and tried to smile, then gave Mom a long kiss on her wet cheek. Slowly I turned away.

It took forever for the door to slide open.

I walked down the hall to the open elevator, stepped inside, and turned around to look back. Dad had his arm around Mom, and suddenly I wished very hard that they would solve their problems and stay together.

"Sure you don't want us to come to the airport with you?" Mom called out.

I shook my head. They waved as the door closed, and

I dropped toward the street, feeling lost and alone, dis-liking myself for being so soft as I held back tears.

Thoughts of Marisa distracted me as the subway shot through the boost tube. I had liked her loops of the old Grant Wood landscapes—the leaves fluttering on the trees, the grasses waving, the sun shining into farmhouse windows, the clouds moving in over the horizon like the black soles of a giant's shoes, the rain and lightning flashes. She could create her own animations, good enough to display in shows, not just for covering walls and windows in apartments. Maybe there was a good art school in Hawaii.

Local stations flashed by in the darkness. I tried not to think. "You imagine that you've swallowed every mind around you," Dad had once said, "but there's a lot you don't know." I had felt angry that he should be critical of me for wanting to know things.

"Maybe not all," I had replied, "but much more than you." He had looked at me with his dark-brown eyes, and I couldn't tell whether he was going to laugh or cry. I felt guilty thinking about it. It seemed now that I had expected him to know everything, and had been dis-appointed when I found out otherwise. I should have told him how excited I was about the things I was learn-ing; and he should have taken more of an interest in what I was doing, shown more appreciation, something he had never done. I realized now that he felt bad about it, that he knew his chance to have been a better father was gone, but it was too late.

Memory is a bridge to the past, and to the future. Each of my earlier selves had been looking forward to me, pushing me across that bridge as I worked to do what they had only dreamed; but I had to build each section of the bridge as I went, just to have a place to go. What worried me was that I couldn't see myself on the other side. Maybe no one could do that, because the bridge was everything, and we all betray our past selves.

Who was I looking forward to being? Suddenly I knew what I was afraid of: I would be making my own mistakes now. Mom and Dad had made quite a few. Who was I to think that I would do better? But I had to do better, I told myself. It was a pact I had made with my earlier selves. I would never forget anything, and that would make the difference.

Then it hit me again that I was leaving *everything*, my parents, New York, Earth. Nothing would be the same again.

The boost train glided into Kennedy-Air and slowed to a stop. I sat there for a minute, getting a grip on my fears and doubts.

Morey boarded the shuttle from New York to Brazil's Equatorial Spaceport and marched down the aisle to where I sat, about halfway in.

He sat down roughly, nudging me with his elbow, but I was glad to have a friend going with me.

"I'm happy that's over," he said. "My parents wanted to come down to the spaceport with me. I had to talk them out of it. They came down here, though. Sorry I'm late."

"That's okay, you made it."

We fastened our seat belts and watched the small screens on the backs of the seats in front of us. The shuttle began to move. Towers, hangars, the hotels and swirling walkways of Kennedy-Air rushed by as the view switched forward, right, left, and rear, running through its endless routine.

We went up, climbing until the sky turned deep blue. A hundred and ten kilometers up, the craft turned off its engines and glided south. I'd been on air shuttles before, but the moment of engine shut-off always took my breath away.

Stars burned in the purple-black over Africa as we whispered toward the equator, and the curving horizon made me feel the smallness of the planet. I was used to thinking of New York State as a suburb of New York City, but at this altitude a shuttle could reach Cairo, or any city on the globe, within an hour; you had to leave the planet to go anywhere far. Soon now, I realized, I would get a taste of *real* distance for the first time—from here to the Moon's orbit; and yet that was a local run compared to interplanetary distances,— to Mars or Mercury, for example.

I touched a control on my armrest and called up a view of deep space. People lived out in that black sky—on the Moon, Mercury, Mars, in the Asteroid Belt, and on the moons of Jupiter and Saturn; two million in the Bernal Clusters alone, more in the O'Neill Cylinders of Sun Orbit, not to mention the ten thousand dockworkers of the Asteroid Hollow in High Earth Orbit, where the giant artificial caves served as berths for the massive interplanetary ships.

I dreamed of faraway worlds with strange skies. Domed cities on Mars and Venus, underground bases on Titan and Pluto, people looking outward to the nearer stars—to the triple system of Alpha Centauri, only four light-years away. I raced across the wispy clouds below, outrunning the shuttle to Earth's edge, where I gazed out into the starry blaze of the galaxy and forgot all my doubts.

Deep space. Sunspace was just a backyard compared with what lay out there. Yet I could blot out a million suns with my hand. The thought of going out there, of becoming even a small part of humanity's Sunspace Settlements, sent a happy chill up my back, and I was no longer afraid.

What appealed to me most was that the rest of the solar system had not been *given* to humankind; people like me had gone out there to build and transform worlds for themselves. It seemed *right* to be able to do that, so much more human and creative than to be handed a world at birth by nature.

"What is it?" Morey asked.

"Just thinking. Neat, isn't it?"

"It's very beautiful," he said softly.

Clouds floated up and covered our screens; then the shuttle fell through into sunlight, and the sight of the world below filled me with wonder.

Blue-green jungle covered Earth. We were in the final approach glide to Clarke Equatorial Spaceport.

"Take it easy," Morey said. "We haven't even left the planet yet." But I could tell that he was also excited.

The big screen at the front of the aisle flashed:

June 29, 2056, 2:02 P.M.
ETA: 2:10 P.M.

Morey and I tightened our seat belts. The screens showed the spaceport ahead—square after square of cleared land covered with buildings, hangars, roads and walkways, and spacecraft crouching on launchpads. Earth's spin being fastest here on the equator—sixteen hundred kilometers per hour—it was most economical to use that extra push to throw vehicles into orbit.

Almost every kind of launch system had been tried here, from complex stage rockets belching chemical propellent to track catapults to laser-fed and atomic rockets; various versions of these systems were still operational. There had even been a plan to run a cable elevator from an island out in the South Atlantic to an asteroid satellite in High Earth Orbit. That would have been awesome— a bridge disappearing into the sky—but the scheme had been abandoned for various technical, political, and safety reasons, even though it might have been successful if enough people had persisted.

The new gravitic catapult had come along in time to make most other systems obsolete. I was eager to see it in action. Maybe our flight was going to use it, I thought excitedly.

We were very low now. I tensed as the craft touched the runway and the feeling of free fall faded from my stomach. The shuttle slowed, but slow was still very fast; the ship covered several miles before coming to a halt.

"We're here," Morey said. He seemed a bit shaky as he unclipped his belt and stood up.

"What is it?" I asked.

"Upset stomach. It's going away."

I got up, and again I realized that we had come to a place that sent people through the sky into the blackness beyond Earth. The thought struck me in the most stupidly obvious way, and I teetered on the edge between excitement and fear as I followed Morey to the exit and out into a long tunnel.

At the end of the passage we put our cards into the

passport check and pressed our palms down on the scan. Our cards popped back; we took them and went out into the waiting area, and it seemed to me suddenly that my whole previous life lay a hundred years or more behind me. I was free forever of the things I had worried about yesterday.

The sun and countryside were visible through the massive dome of the waiting area. Temperatures outside were probably over forty centigrade. The rain forest pressed in around the spaceport, and I thought of it as a sleeping thing that dreamed its animals, insects, flowers, and greenery; but it could not have dreamed the spaceport; we had done that ourselves, and I wondered if the forest were jealous.

Hundreds of people filled the great floor of the terminal, waiting to depart for all parts of Sunspace. Some stood by their luggage. Many were well dressed; others looked poorer. I noticed a group dressed in gray uniforms with red armbands.

"Convicts," Morey said. "Probably shipping out for the mining towns of the Belt."

I stared at their glum faces. One young woman gave me a loutish look. Earth had turned against them. It was a sure way of making certain that a criminal would not repeat his crime anywhere near where he was sentenced.

"They'll probably never come back," Morey said softly. "It's sad."

"Happens all the time," Morey replied.

A muffled roar startled me. I looked up and saw a ship cross the Sun's face, rising on vertical turbojets. Its nuclear pulse engine would ignite in the upper atmosphere and push the vessel away from Earth with a steady acceleration. The reality of it rushed through me like a jolt of electricity. Such ships and their larger cousins crossed the trillion-kilometer whirlpool of sun and planets in a few weeks. And the new gravity launchers would hurl them off the planet even more economically.

A three-dee sign flashed in my eyes:

ORBITAL TOURS!
SIGN NOW!

I blinked nervously and saw a holo of Earth from Low Orbit; then one from High Orbit. Elephants and human shapes tumbled through the void. Power satellites beamed energy down through the atmosphere, serviced by stubby robots and toy figures in spacesuits.

BECOME A SUNSPACER!
HIGH PAY AND A SCENIC PLACE TO LIVE!
PLUMBERS, ELECTRICIANS, VEHICLE AND
STRUCTURAL MAINTENANCE SKILLS NEEDED!
TEACHERS WELCOME!
APPRENTICE APPLICATIONS AVAILABLE
FOR ALL JOBS!

To many people Clarke Station was probably just another travel terminal, even though people were going
home to Marsport, to the Moon, or to places that had
only coordinates in space for an address; but for me it
was all new suddenly, as if it had begun yesterday morning. Maybe I was taking my mind off the big change in
my life, but I didn't care; our solar civilization was big
and growing bigger, and I was going out to see its true
size. I wanted to cheer. There were millions of people
out there, and they thought of themselves as being from
space in the same way I thought of New York City as
home. And somewhere in the terminal there was probably a Sunspacer who was coming to Earth to study, and
feeling just as excited as I was to be leaving.

"Come on," Morey said.

I followed him, imagining a whole civilization in space,
thousands of space habitats, millions of people eating
and drinking, going to school, raising children, playing,
thinking, and feeling, dreaming about the stars. One
day the free habitats would scatter out into the spiral
arms of the galaxy in search of resources and knowledge.

I was going out there, and maybe I would help make
it happen. I tried to picture the reality of off-planet life;
it was something I had always taken for granted, but
now I was going to see it for myself.

"It's neat," I said, walking next to Morey.

"What is?"

"All this, here, and where we're going."

"It's not so neat," he said. "It could be much better."

I didn't know quite what he meant, but he didn't seem to care whether I understood or not. "It doesn't seem possible that human beings could have done it all," I said.

"Well it wasn't just given to us one Christmas."

"I know we built it," I said stupidly. "Human beings, I mean."

He stopped and looked at me. We put down our bags. "You really want to know? All this happened because of a small group of people with pencils and paper—the theoretical physicists and chemists of the last five centuries. The engineers and builders applied their work, but it was all really finished a long time ago. We're still catching up with the theoreticians."

"Well, sure, I know. But the builders still had to make it all *real*."

He shrugged and picked up his bag. "They'd have nothing to do without all the *hard* work being done for them. We'd still be riding horses."

I couldn't get upset at what he was saying, not just then; he wanted to become a theoretical physicist, after all. I imagined a team of white horses pulling a giant wagon through space. The driver was cracking a whip and shouting at the stars. It didn't bother me that he wasn't wearing a spacesuit; neither were the horses.

4 THROUGH THE SKY

The inscription on the giant block of stainless steel in the center of the terminal floor read:

E q u a t o r i a l   S p a c e p o r t   1

OPENED FOR THE PEOPLE OF EARTH
1996

THE STEEL IN THIS MEMORIAL WAS MANUFAC-
TURED OUT OF ORES MINED FROM THE FIRST
ASTEROID BROUGHT INTO EARTH ORBIT

2018

"Ten minutes to boarding," Morey said, sending another chill of expectation up my back. We were really going; it wasn't just something we were talking about.

I heard a muffled, crackling roar, and looked up in time to see a stubby orbiter rising on a red laser column. The beam tracked the ship, pumping energy into its engines. As the orbiter grew small and disappeared, I imagined its rising arc over the South Atlantic. The laser winked off as the craft attained enough speed to make orbit.

"We can look around some," Morey said in the sudden quiet.

Human beings were aliens on the equator, I thought as we began to explore the interconnecting domes; the heat and humidity outside could kill.

The first dome we entered was filled with recruiting booths. Flashing holo signs hurried us to join in the building of new worlds:

FIND YOURSELF!
IN EXCITING WORK!

Spacescapes revealed distant parts of the solar system. The three-dee images produced vivid afterimages in my visual field. I was beginning to dislike being seized by the throat to get my attention.

"Now boarding!" a male voice boomed. "Shuttle 334 for Bernal One!"

"Didn't your folks want to come and see you off?" Morey asked as we waited on line.

I shook my head and felt sorry for myself. "They didn't even come to graduation."

"What? I thought they were there."

"I didn't want to bring it up. It doesn't matter."

"What happened?"

"Nothing much. They had a fight and were out of town."

There were a few people our age on the line, and I wondered if they were also going away to school.

"Parents think they'll have you around forever," Morey said as the line began to move forward. "Then they crack up when the time runs out and they realize they can't make up for anything."

I took a deep breath. "It was more than that, Morey. They're breaking up. Dad wanted the usual renewal and Mom just wouldn't give him one. It's their problem now."

"Well, it happens." He glanced at me. "I'm sorry, Joe."

"Bernal One!" the same male voice announced. "Last call!"

This was it. I was going out there, into the darkness of space, protected only by the shuttle.

"Didn't you have a bag?" Morey asked as the line moved through the tunnel.

I looked around, not really caring. "Must have left it somewhere. They'll send it home to my parents. I can do without that stuff."

"Got your wallet?" Morey asked, grinning.

"Sure, right here."

"Credit codes?"

"I never forget."

We came out of the tunnel and boarded the tube car that would take us to the pad, two miles away. I grabbed a window seat and stared outside. It was the first time for both of us, and I wondered why Morey wasn't as excited as I was; maybe Aristotle was right—knowledge killed the sense of wonder in the knower.

The car slid forward and shot into the darkness. I turned away from the window and looked around the brightly lit inside, wondering if I would get to know any of the faces at school. Most of the girls were alone, as were the boys. Only one girl was with an older woman, but she could have been a sister. One boy seemed to be with both parents, and he was looking uneasy.

The car glided out into a brightly lit area and slowed to a stop. Somewhere above us was the gravitic shuttle, waiting to carry us through the sky.

"How's the stomach?" I asked Morey.

"All better," he said as we stood up.

Emerging out onto a platform, we took our places on the line in front of the elevator.

"Attention please!"

A young man appeared at our right, hands on hips. He seemed to me to be looking at us critically.

"I'm your guide. My name is Kik ten Eyck," he announced loudly. "I'll be with you until we reach the college." I thought he sounded as if he were herding a bunch of sheep. "I'll be around to answer your questions and help you with any problems." It was just a job to him, it seemed. Deliver the Earthies, dump them in the dorm, and get paid. His casual manner was probably fine for very nervous types. The flight was no big thing for him, and that would calm some people, but he seemed arrogant to me.

When our turn came, Morey and I stepped into the lift with half a dozen other kids and were whisked up the ship's center to our seats.

Seats 22 and 23 were a third of the way to the nose. I grabbed the window seat again, but it didn't matter; as in the air shuttle, there was no port, only a small screen on the overhead partition. It made for a safer ship, allowing for extra shielding from radiation and meteors.

"It's bigger than I thought," Morey said, peering up the shaft.

The empty lift went down past us. "Please fasten your seat belts." In the confined space the voice sounded as if it were talking in my ear. I sat back and looked up at the screen.

It lit up, showing a crisscross of black roads, with weeds in between. "The launch plate," the woman's voice continued, "is a finely tuned installation that must be protected from heat and dust." The weeds moved as the cover was pulled back, and the launcher emerged from below ground, a metal tube with a silvery ship standing halfway out of it, ready to pierce the sky.

I heard a high whining sound. My arms began to feel heavier. It seemed strange to be watching the ship I was in.

"Gravity inside the ship," the woman's voice went on, "will increase to six times normal before the shuttle is released by the reversing field."

The high-pitched sound grew louder. Vast amounts of power were flowing in to create the repelling g force. Our seats adjusted to face the overhead screen. I felt myself being pressed back into the heavy cushioning.

"I feel like an elephant," Morey said.

The blue sky on the screen shimmered from the singing sound. A strange, hurrying happiness filled me.

I was the ship as it went up. A burst of yellow-orange sunlight struck my eyes; weightless, I fell toward a blue ocean of sky. . . .

It was strange to see a spacecraft lifting without a laser or jets, rising but also dropping away from Earth, since a reversed gravitational field was involved. An invisible cone of negative gravity was pushing the vessel up to the speed needed to reach the Moon's orbit.

The ship climbed through the sky, fleeing the piercing cry of the launcher, becoming a small needle on the screen, held in a gravitational vise between heaven and earth.

I fell back into myself as the picture blinked and we saw a three-dee view of Brazil next to a sparkling ocean;

the holo blinked again, showing stars and the glowing, deep-violet curve of the planetary horizon. We were coming out of an ocean of air into the splendor of Sunspace, pushed outward from the cradle of life by the mirror image of Earth's own attraction. The ship had its own maneuvering engines, of course, but the short passage to Lunar Orbit did not require a fully powered trajectory. We would be in the weightlessness of free fall all the way to the Bernal Cluster.

"We'll be reaching a speed of eighty thousand kilometers per hour," the whispery voice said, "but allowing for slowing and maneuvering, the journey will take about twelve hours. Enjoy your trip and use caution in moving around. Zero-g pills will be dispensed by the steward to those passengers who may need them." The voice seemed to chuckle for an instant.

"May I help you?" a steward asked from the passageway.

Morey grabbed the pills and swallowed them with water from a squeezeball. I hadn't noticed how sick he had become.

The steward looked at me. "How about you?"

"No, thanks," I said, even though my stomach gurgled a bit.

"You'd better," he insisted.

I took the pills and forced down the water, noticing that Morey seemed a bit relieved that I wasn't immune.

He had obviously been trying to hide his discomfort ever since the air shuttle.

"Thanks," Morey said, passing my squeezeball back to the steward.

"I'm Jake LeStrange. I'll be here if you need me. If you want a snack or drink, just push the button. The slots aren't working yet." He spoke with his lips close together, as if he had something in his mouth. His hair was cut down to a stubble on his skull; some of it seemed gray, but he looked young.

"No food," Morey said. "Don't even mention it."

"Barf bags are here," Jake said, pointing, and floated away.

Morey took a deep breath. "I see this . . . mess sloshing in my gut. Hope you're not going to eat anything."

"I don't feel too good myself," I said, even though I was actually feeling much better than Morey.

Stars showed on the screen. Earth's sky was behind us.

"You may have a more direct experience, if you wish," the whispery voice said, "by using the personal viewer." A slot opened under the screen. I pulled out the gogglelike viewer on its cable.

"Want to look?" I asked Morey.

"Not now."

I put it on and looked out through the ship's eyes, into a deep blackness filled with stars. It was not the

same as looking at a holoscreen; this was three-dee without a frame. I was out in space without a suit, yet safe
from the heat and cold and lack of air.

I looked back at Earth and saw the glow of its atmosphere, that protective membrane which filtered sunlight down to just the right intensity. The planet seemed
safe and peaceful, a good firm place to put your feet.
Of course, it was a safe home only because we had adapted
to the amounts of sunlight it received, though not perfectly; we could stand up in its gravity and breathe the
air, though not without some difficulties. The planet was
safe, except for natural disasters, which still killed too
many people.

But life had a good chance on Earth. It was still the
main home of humankind, and a better place than it
had been during the twentieth century, when irrespon-
sible forms of technology and industrialization had en-
dangered the whole planet, even while making it possible
to support the largest number of people in all history.

Things had improved when people had pioneered
Sunspace, gradually taking the dirtiest industries out
into that vastness of resources and the Sun's streaming
energy. Earth was recovering because people had learned
to see it as I was now seeing it, as only *one* place, not the
whole universe.

Earth was a huge organism, alive because death was
part of its recycling system. I don't think human beings
had ever forgiven it that, as much as they tried to love

nature. The last century and a half had seen the con-
quest of the air, the splitting of the atom, the settling of
space, and a continuous attack on disease and death.
But we could never be sentimental about nature again.
The rebellious skills of civilization kept us alive on Earth
and beyond it.

Some Sunspacers claimed that they wouldn't need Earth
at all in time, that it was the home of a dying culture,
holding humanity back from the stars. It wouldn't matter in the long run, I thought, watching cities wink on
their lights as darkness crept across the globe. Earth and
the Sunspace Settlements were doing well, so it had to
be pride and cultural rivalry. No, that wasn't completely
it, I thought, remembering the real grievances of the
miners on Mercury, as well as the sense of growing economic dependence that Earth felt toward off-worlders.

The view made a full turn, giving me the illusion of
my head turning around on my shoulders. The Sun
swept by—toned down to protect my eyes—our own
magnificent hearth-fire in a cave of stars; the Moon's
silvery face sailed into view. I heard Morey throwing up
at my left, but I didn't want to embarrass him, so I kept
the goggles on, marveling at the dense starfields beyond
our solar system.

Morey and I found out that we had to strap down
fairly tightly in order to sleep in zero-g, to keep from
drifting even a little. There were those, I learned later,

who liked to sleep with loose straps, floating a bit; some liked to float free completely. I was too new at it to have a preference.

Unable to sleep deeply, I floated over Morey, who was asleep with hands gripping the armrests, and drifted out into the passageway. Slowly, I pulled myself along to the men's washroom in the midsection. Suddenly it seemed that the nose was the bottom of a long drop. I cried out, expecting to fall.

Jake LeStrange was in the small lounge, drifting against one wall, dragging on a cigarette. He looked bored when I floated in.

"Hi, kid. Can't sleep?"

"Guess not." I didn't like the "kid" bit.

"It's common the first time. Later you can't wake them. Reminds them of being in Mommy's belly."

"Really?" I asked sarcastically.

He scratched his shaved scalp. "Something you want, kid? The toilet's in there. Read the instructions before you let loose."

"Thanks, I think I can figure it out."

He grinned.

I didn't like him, I decided as I drifted into the enclosure and slid the door shut. Sunspacers and earthies just weren't always going to get along, I realized, wondering how much was my fault, if any.

A jungle of graffiti grew on the walls. A few lines caught my eye:

44

Principal products: Moon—green
cheese.
Mars—red sand.
Earth—salt water.

The meek shall inherit the Earth.
They can have it!
The rest of us are going somewhere else.

Watch out for the coriolis force on Bernal.
Wear a mask when you pee!

Most of the others were just as dumb, or confusing. Pride lay behind the words, misunderstanding, as well as political and economic grievances that would have to be settled before real hatred took hold. Maybe it was already too late; no one was sure what would happen if the miners on Mercury went on strike, as they were threatening. Earth was importing too much from Space to ignore the possibility of major shortages. It seemed to me that the Sunspacers were doing a lot, and not getting as much respect for it as they would have wished.

I wondered if Jake might have written all the graffiti, since they all seemed to have been printed by the same hand. It wouldn't have surprised me.

I opened one eye. The Moon was on the screen.

"Breakfast in ten minutes," the whispery voice said. "Open your slot and remove the contents while they are still hot. Put everything back when you are finished and please make sure the cover is closed." The voice sounded half asleep and bored with reading the instructions for the thousandth time.

"We'll be docking at Bernal One early this afternoon," it continued. "Have a pleasant morning and be careful when moving around."

I heard a laugh. Jake was floating in the passage. "What she never says is how many people have broken their necks in zero-g."

"Thanks for telling us," I said sarcastically, hoping he would go away. Morey was waking up.

"Sure," Jake went on. "They think because they're weightless their heads don't have any *mass* either." He chuckled as he held on to the handbar, sounding as if he were gargling saliva. He probably tried these stories on anyone who would listen.

"Who's the voice?" I asked.

"Sylvia's the copilot. You should hear her when she's been up a week."

Morey opened his eyes, looking angry. "Do you mind? We're just getting up."

Jake slid the divider shut.

"A pest," Morey said.

"Sure is. How do you feel?" He looked pale.

"My circulation feels bad. I get dizzy." He focused and looked at me. "How about you?"

"Okay, I guess. Sometimes I get the feeling that we're falling in that direction." I pointed toward the nose.

He grunted. "That's exactly what we're doing."

"Breakfast," I said. The light was on over the utility slot. I brought up my seat, slid open the panel, and reached in for the tray. It was hot in the small space. Morey drew up his seat as I took out the tray and placed it on his magnetic handrests. Everything on the tray was held down by stickstrips. I took out my tray and sat back, held in place by the strap.

Coffee and juice came in suck tubes; oatmeal in a big squeeze bulb; scrambled eggs and ham in a widemouth bulb.

Our divider slid open halfway. "Food okay?" Jake asked.

Morey nodded.

Jake looked at me.

"It's okay."

"It used to really stink," Jake said, floating away.

"Feel better?" I asked as we continued eating. There was some color in Morey's face now.

"I think so."

He stretched and yawned when he was finished. I got rid of the trays.

"Thanks," he said, staring sadly at the screen, as if he were trying to remember something.

"What is it?" I was beginning to worry about him.

"Earth is so small."

"It happens when you go far away from something."

"It looks lost," he said, ignoring my joke. "We're leaving everything behind. Most of what has happened to human beings happened *there*."

"Yeah, I know," I said, trying to sound sympathetic. I thought of all the windows I had broken in the condemned sections of Westchester before we moved to Manhattan. I wondered if Willy, my fellow destroyer, still lived there. The area had been rebuilt into a residential arcology, housing a half million people in a tall pyramid, and the new windows were unbreakable.

"There's more than Earth now," I said. "We're not all in one place, but I know how you feel. I was thinking the same things about four o'clock this morning."

"I'll miss the pizzamat near my house," Morey said.

"Don't worry. As long as you can order the same recipe on Bernal, it'll be just the same."

At 2:31 in the afternoon, Bernal One slid into view on the screen—a huge ball with what looked like tire tubes piled up on its north and south poles.

"Please strap in," Sylvia said.

The ship was turning for its approach as Morey and I buckled in.

Bernal One grew larger, but it sure didn't look sixteen kilometers across, or as if fifty thousand or more people

48

could be living inside; but there was nothing in our field of view with which to compare it.

Braking thrusters fired, pressing us into our cushions. We came in high over Bernal's north pole, then twisted slowly to face down into the hole of stacked tires, which now looked more like doughnuts, where the open docks were located. The ship made minor corrections as we drifted into the mouth. I caught sight of several space-suited figures making repairs outside with welding torches. Bernal settled down on us, obliterating the stars as we drifted inside and nudged to a halt.

Morey smiled at me. "Well, we made it."

"Routine, almost dull," I said, not meaning it.

"Sure," Morey replied, sounding much better.

People drifted past us in the passage. Morey and I unstrapped and joined the flow, pulling ourselves along the handbars to the rear exit, where we floated out into a large, drum-shaped zero-g space. Handrails criss-crossed this interior, snaking in and out of openings. About a hundred people were waiting, hanging on the rails like so many coats on a rack.

Kik ten Eyck darted in through an entrance at my right, and stopped where the rails crossed in the center.

"You'll go inside in small groups," he said loudly, "and your counselor will take you as far as the dorms." He looked around at us for a moment, then shot out of the chamber.

"Some service," Morey said, looking pale again.

A girl floated toward us after a few minutes. She was dressed in a white leotard, brown shorts, and stickboots. Her red hair was braided and piled on top of her head. I guessed that she was about twenty.

"Hello," she said, attaching herself to the drum wall with her boots. "I'm Linda ten Eyck. We'll be entering the biosphere through its north pole, the same zero-g axis along which you docked. Your sense of weight will increase as we move off that axis toward the equator, where it will feel almost Earth normal. Remember, 'gravity' here is really centrifugal force, so *try* not to trip over your feet, and don't *jump*. It's not too dangerous, but you may not land *exactly* where you expect. Even a sphere rotation of less than once a minute can't reproduce the perfect illusion of a genuine gravitational field. Oh, one more thing. Going through zones of varying gravity may temporarily affect your balance, but don't worry. Most people get their space legs quick."

I was watching her as she gave her talk. Her green eyes were a bit slanted. She was younger than I had first thought, maybe my age; self-confidence made her seem older.

"Let's go," she said, and launched herself across the drum. Morey and I crept along the rail. What if I couldn't adapt? Maybe I had a fussy inner ear that knew how to balance only on Earth. I was a little worried about Morey again; she had implied that there were people who couldn't adjust.

"This way!" she called without looking back. Her body was slim, but I noticed a surprising roundness in her hips as she jackknifed and slipped into the exit.

"She's probably ten Eyck's sister," Morey said as we pulled through after her.

"That's right." The name had gone right past me.

Suddenly we were floating straight up on a cushion of air. Linda was waiting halfway to the top of the tunnel. White light shone across her body. I heard Morey breathing next to me as we drifted up level with her.

"In here," she said, seeming impatient, and I felt that she thought me hopelessly clumsy. We drifted by her, into what looked like a rail car. The top was transparent, and there were large windows on the sides.

Morey and I pulled ourselves down into two empty seats near the back.

"Buckle in," Linda said loudly. I noticed another car ahead of ours. Both were now full.

"At least the seats look upright," a man said to his son in the seat in front of us.

"It doesn't matter," I said, buckling in. "We could be sitting on the ceiling and it wouldn't matter." The man turned and looked at us, then turned away, and I realized that it had not been necessary for me to share my knowledge. I was excited by our arrival, and a bit worried about Morey.

A few students looked confused. One father was holding his son's hand. I caught a glimpse of Linda in the front car. She seemed amused as the vehicle moved forward.

I peered out into the darkness of the tunnel. We slipped suddenly into daylight. A hollow world curved away in all directions, closing into a ball at the south pole, far below the ring of sunlight on the other side of the equator.

I didn't know much then about the system of mirrors and windows that brought sunlight into the colony, so it was hard to make perfect sense of what I was seeing. We were attached to our seats, heads pointing to the center of a great hollow ball. Suddenly it seemed I was looking *down* at everything.

"There's some weight," Morey said with relief. The illusion of looking down was gone. Morey took a deep breath. "Fresh air and greenery."

The cars ran on a monorail that gradually left the zero-g axis, delivering passengers from the space dock to the inner surface. The hollow ball was a giant centrifuge. Its spin threw you out from the center, but the inner surface was there to stop you, so it felt almost like gravity to your feet. Put a bucket of water on the end of a rope, whirl it around fast, and the water will stay inside. Not gravity, but just as good where you can't get any. I couldn't feel the difference.

Looking back, I saw the tunnel mouth rising away from us as we moved along the curved surface. I faced forward and looked around for Linda, but she had disappeared.

"Your sense of weight," her voice said suddenly over the speaker, "will increase as we near the equatorial zone. You can see the university ahead, to the right of the lake."

Again it seemed that I was looking down through a giant balloon. "Look at that!" I said, nudging Morey, but he had closed his eyes. Then the perspective reversed itself, and it seemed that we were traveling uphill toward the lake; but I was still getting flashes of downhill motion. Things started to look more normal when I stopped thinking about it and simply accepted the direction of my feet as down. After that the curve of the landscape was just an exotic detail.

I looked at Morey. He still seemed pale, but his eyes were open and he was looking around. I was glad.

"Feeling better?"

"I'll be okay," he said, still looking a bit embarrassed. "How about you?"

"Great. Can't wait to get outside."

5 BERNAL HALL

I began to feel heavier as the monorail slipped toward the equator. Looking up, I saw a pedal glider moving across the bright open space of the globe. "That's not a dead-stick glider," Linda's voice explained. "It's a human-powered aircraft with a propeller." Far to my right, a group of people seemed to be playing football, except that they were highjumping and somersaulting in low gravity.

Everywhere I looked there were houses—old and new designs, two and three stories high, some of them looking as if they had been snatched off twentieth-century Earth, or earlier, and attached to the inner surface of the hollow sphere. Country roads passed slyly in and out of forested areas. The equatorial lake spilled a river around the world; streams branched from the main flow; small bridges straddled the waterways; people were everywhere, accepting their world in the ordinary way.

It was ordinary to them, but it couldn't be that for

me, not yet anyway, if ever. It filled me up with its reality, its impossible neatness and order. I couldn't believe that we were traveling to a dorm room; everything would be different here, even beds, desks, and bathrooms. I was *inside* a world on the other side of the sky; a few centuries ago that would have meant that I had died and gone to heaven.

"Many people from Earth," Linda's voice continued over the speaker, "have the idea that space habitats are small, cramped places . . ."

"We're not *that* uninformed," Morey said sourly.

It still seemed to me that Dandridge Cole University lay at the bottom of a hill, but the angle was flattening out. I saw circles of buildings on the left shore of the lake.

". . . and that's the park in the center," Linda was saying. "Dorms in the inner circle, classrooms in the middle one. The outer ring is for research and advanced studies. Agriculture's in the farm toruses—those doughnuts stacked on the outside, which you saw during docking."

I turned and looked back at the north, then south again. The poles were the holes in the hollow tires, opening into the worlds of the toruses.

"Can't you sit still?" Morey asked.

I leaned forward and peered toward the ring of sunlight around the south pole. Bridges crossed the brightness. Just then we glided over a river of light, and I realized that this was the northern sun circle. A glowing band curved away left and right.

"A circle of windows with exterior mirrors," Linda said, "which cast light inside . . ."

"She's so thrilled," Morey said.

I looked at him with disdain. "What's the matter?"

"I'll be fine."

He still wasn't, but he wasn't going to admit it.

The landscape seemed to become more level as we neared the equator. Even inside a hollow ball, a diameter of sixteen kilometers will give some sensation of flatness when you're not looking across a large distance; there's no way to hide the fact that you're inside a hollow ball, that people are going about their business at right angles to you, and overhead, but in time you do accept the rightness of it. It couldn't be otherwise once you understood the conditions; the same thing is true of Earth.

The big lake glistened at our right as we rushed over a stream and entered the outer ring of the University. Here the research buildings were three-story drum shapes with curving window bands. Greenery flashed by and we were among the classroom structures—two-floor saucers, single-level rectangles, domes, and ovals. Students hurried along walkways and sat on benches.

I caught sight of a large group carrying electronic signs. The scene went by fast, but I was able to read three of the displays:

END DEATH ON MERCURY!
FREE THE MINERS!
EARTH'S SHAME!

"Did you see that?" I asked Morey.

He nodded and shrugged. "Politics. Some people never outgrow it."

His answer irritated me. "But you know it's a just cause. You've said so yourself."

Another green area flashed past and I saw the dorms—three-floor red brick-patterned drums with window bands like those in the research ring.

Morey nodded impatiently. "I know—but in the end it will be the application of *real* power that will bring the settlement. The words of the agreement will just be a rationalization. Those students out there are just the cheering section for one of the power sides."

"I don't care," I said angrily. "What they say is right, isn't it?"

"Sure, nothing can change the truth."

"People should hear it publicly then."

"Coming up," Linda announced, "Bernal Hall, Clarke Hall, Hawking, Ley." She spoke softly, as if something had distracted her. Morey's comments had disturbed me. He was on the right side, but he didn't seem to want to do much about it. Not that I had any idea of what to do, but it seemed to me that one had to be willing to try, at least.

"I have to lie down," Morey said suddenly, the color fading from his face.

"We'll be there in a minute. Hold on."

"Bernal!" Linda shouted as we slowed to a stop. "Watch your step and good luck."

I unbuckled Morey, then myself. "Come on." I stood up.

Morey hoisted himself with a grunt and we went to the forward exit, where we stepped out onto a narrow platform. The cars pulled away.

It was warm outside, reminding me of late spring in rural New York. We wandered down a shallow ramp and found ourselves on a walkway. A sign read:

Bernal Hall

There was no other building at the end of the path, so this castle turret had to be it. As we approached I noticed that Morey and I had two shadows each, one from each Sun ring at the opposite ends of the world.

I stopped and looked up. Morey kept going. "Come on, Joe, I've got to get inside."

"It's like a big map," I said excitedly. The air was crystal clear in the bright sunlight. The buildings, streams, and roadways on the other side of the sphere were very distinct. "It looks farther than I thought it would."

"Come on," Morey said impatiently.

Living all our lives on the outside of a ball so large that people once thought it was flat was no preparation for suddenly moving *inside* a small planet, where the Sun was two hoops of light and the stars were under your feet, on the other side of a gently curving surface. My mind understood this world, but my body had to get used to it day by day; my imagination had to invent the world all over again.

"I feel queasy," Morey said, reminding me that his body was having a tougher time than mine. He took a deep breath and turned to go inside.

"You'll get used to it," I said, catching up to him. "I know you will." Suddenly I was afraid that he would have to go back to Earth.

A side door opened for us and we went in, stepping into a brightly lit hallway that curved away to the right.

"It should be on this floor," I said as we counted off the numbers from 112 down. There was a sign on 108:

Joseph G. Sorby
Morey Green-Wolfe

I didn't like the formal look the middle initial gave my name.

"Here's us," I said, pressing my palm against the lock ID.

The door slid open; lights and ventilation cut in as we stepped inside. Morey sat down on the bunk that stood against the left wall. He gulped air for a moment, then struggled to his feet and staggered to the door. It slid open and he shuffled out toward the bathroom down the hall.

The phone on the right-hand desk buzzed. I sat down and thumbed the line open, wondering if this set was cued to my ID. Dad's face appeared on the small screen, making me feel that I hadn't gone very far from home at all.

"Well, you made it," he said after the usual three-second round-trip delay in the signal. "Good trip?"

"It was okay."

"I should have come with you," he said after a moment. "Why didn't you tell me about the picnic for parents and students? You'll go anyway, won't you?"

That made me angry. It was easy for him to be sorry now. "It was *your* business to know," I said, and waited.

"You're right," he said after the dead spot. "Got your money codes?"

I nodded. "Look, I've got to unpack, get sheets and stuff."

"Don't use more credit without telling me first. Call when you want, on me. Leave a message if there's no answer."

Yellow flowers dotted the lawn outside my window.

Nearby dorms were chocolate cakes with silver windows for frosting.

Dad sniffed. I knew he was feeling guilty, but I didn't care.

"How's Morey?"

"A little sick, but he'll get over it."

"Will you come home for holidays, or should we come out there?"

"I don't know yet."

The delay seemed longer as I struggled to control my resentment.

"Glad to be out there?"

"Sure."

"Well," he said after the pause, "it seems right for you, and that's important. I'm sure you'll do well." *Be glad you got what you wanted,* he was really saying, *but you're on your own.*

I nodded, unable to say anything. Finally I forced a smile.

"Good luck, son," he said, biting his lower lip. "Eva will call you in a few days."

The picture went dark. I sat there, telling myself that I should have let him have it when it would have hurt the most, because he had called to make himself feel better. I got up after a while and went to look for Morey.

Mom would have wanted me to have a private bath, I thought as I came to the double doors and was let into a large square room with a dozen sinks, showers, and toilet stalls. She wouldn't have liked the small phone screen either, but I didn't care; I wouldn't have to do any cleaning, so it was worth it.

"Joe?" Morey asked from the end stall. He wasn't improving the atmosphere any. I almost had to hold my nose.

"What is it?"

"I'm still not feeling better."

"You want a medic?" I'd never heard him sound so down.

"Maybe I'm imagining too much. My mind knows it's not real gravity, so I keep thinking about the spin that holds me down."

"Forget it."

"I'm glad my parents aren't here. Mom would say my tummy has the whoopsies and Dad would say, gee—this whole place spins, and Mom would suggest that maybe I shouldn't stay at all. . . ."

"Going to the picnic?" I asked.

"How can I?"

"I'll keep you company. But not in here."

I went out through the sliding doors and wandered back to the room. My lost bag was on my trunk. I checked the address label and saw that it had been changed to my new address—by Mom, probably. Unpacking would make an exciting afternoon, I thought, still feeling a bit angry and depressed. I wasn't really here yet, I realized. I wanted to be here, but I was still back on Earth.

I sat down at my desk and examined the library link, noticing the portable screen for those who might like to work in out-of-the-way places. I gazed out the window at the hill that fell away to my right. The tall grass would be a great place to lie down and read. I wandered over to my bed and lay down, realizing that I hadn't escaped anything; there would be new problems here, and the old ones would continue to visit, as long as there were phones and I was still Joe Sorby.

I would have to become someone else.

Silvery light filtered in through the window when I opened my eyes. Morey's dark shape stood over me.

"What's the time?"

"About midnight," he said.

"Fell asleep," I mumbled, sitting up slowly.

"They gave me something at the infirmary, so I went over to the picnic."

"Why didn't you wake me?"

"You looked so peaceful, like you needed it. You didn't want to go anyway."

"What was it like?"

"The university president spoke, telling us that more people from Earth should visit the Sunspace Settlements to promote better understanding of where the future lay for our civilization—off-planet. There was a demonstration for the miners on Mercury. It didn't last long. A lot of students seem to be involved in the cause." He sounded impressed and a bit uncertain.

I sat up on the edge of the bed and rubbed my eyes. "The trip tired me more than I thought."

"You're a bit sick from the changeover. People react differently, they said at the infirmary."

"What's that light outside?"

"The mirrors bring in moonlight same as the Sun."

"I don't remember falling asleep."

"Okay now?"

"Sure."

"Breathe deeply once in a while. I take it the other side of the room is mine."

I nodded. "The phone's coded to me on this side. I missed dinner."

"It was at the picnic."

"Maybe I'll go back to sleep."

"It's a nice night. I'm going for a walk." He gave a crazy laugh, like his usual self. He was obviously relieved to be well again. "It's always a nice night here. How could it not be? They turn it on and off." His dark shape moved toward the door.

"Morey?"

He stopped and turned around, but I couldn't see his face. "What, my friend?" his dark shape asked.

"Are you glad to be here?"

"Now I am, after they fixed me up. Aren't you?"

I was grateful he couldn't see my face in the darkened room. "Sure. Just wanted to know."

The door slid open as I lay down. He went out and it whispered shut. I relaxed in the strange silence and thought of all the space and stars outside the shell— and dreamed I was down in the dorm basement, opening a trap door into the glowing universe outside. The dream was wrong, of course, because the stars were motionless; they should have been moving as Bernal rotated. I fell through the bottom of my new world and drifted away, breathing cold nothing as the naked Sun blistered my face until it looked like a bowl of oatmeal, and I was forced to keep telling people my name because they couldn't recognize me. . . .

6 GETTING SETTLED

There were about fifty students in the dorm's main lounge when Morey and I walked in the next morning. We were given a few once-over stares as we sat down in the back row of the circle of chairs. There was a guy wearing a turban in the front row, sitting next to a couple of slender African women. They towered over him, even sitting down. There was a Japanese kid in the second row who kept turning around and looking past me. Next to him sat a girl with a colorful kerchief over her head. She sat stiffly, as if afraid to look left or right. Suddenly I had the feeling of being trapped, and that nothing was going to be as I had imagined.

There was a loud group of kids at our left, dressed in multicolored metallic sheen shorts and sleeveless shirts. Then I saw Linda ten Eyck with them, and I knew why they sounded so confident; they were all from Bernal or the other settlements—the Sunflower Habitats at L-4 (that's the other Libration Point, one of four such stable areas in the Moon's orbit, equidistant from Earth and Moon), the Moon, Mars, maybe even the Asteroids. They were laughing and talking as if the rest of us didn't exist.

A tall, deeply tanned man came in. There was some gray in his sandy hair, and even more in his beard.

"My name is Bill Turnbull," he said as the chatter quieted, "and I'll be your orientation advisor." He gazed at us with calm gray eyes. "Most of you are physical science majors. That's why you came here, and why you were accepted. You local students can study what you want because we have to take you, but that doesn't mean you can coast. *Anyone* can flunk out, and all the programs are tough. A few major points to keep in mind. Do *not* spend all your time at your desk link, even though you can learn very quickly that way. You are expected to get to know your tutors and classmates." He looked around at us carefully. "Personal growth suffers when you cut yourself off from the lively *connections* made when bright people get together. Use links for busy work, for catch-up, to prepare for discussions with peers and superiors. The *real* goal of your work is not just to know a lot, but to be creative in your area, to contribute to its growth while growing up as a person. All work is for people in the end, even when we benefit ourselves individually." He paused. "If we suspect abuses, we will place a limit on the use of links, and then they will shut down if overused. We've never had to do that."

A tall, thin boy with short black hair stood up three seats to my right. "Does this include talking to other students or teachers? About work, I mean."

Turnbull sighed. "No, but we feel that people are worth talking to personally. It's a Sunspacer value. People are unique presences in the universe, to be held dear."

I liked what Turnbull was saying.

"Anthropocentric prejudice," the boy said with contempt.

"Maybe—but we don't use it for harm. Out here we believe that human life must be at the center of things. Call personal contact our little ceremony, our prayer before a hostile universe, our way of being a community."

Turnbull's words made me feel good, needed. The boy shook his head in amusement and sat down.

"Other questions?"

After a moment of silence, the black-haired boy spoke up again, obviously unable to restrain himself. "Are we here to learn religious dogmas or science? I'm here to study physics, and I don't care about much else, and it's not up to you or anyone to make me care or tell me how to live."

"No one will stop you from doing your work. Don't you have any customs where you come from?"

A short, auburn-haired girl stood up in front of me.

"I think he's just shy and wants to be left alone, but he'll change." I liked her voice and hoped she would turn around.

"What complete nonsense!" the black-haired boy shouted, crossing his legs and leaning back. "Next you'll tell us we have to join the marches for those miners on Merk."

"What's your name?" Turnbull asked.

"Christopher Van Cott. Does it go on a list of baddies?"

"Where you from, Chris?"

"Chicago Arc One. And it's Christopher."

"You know, Christopher, there are few real loners in science. It's a cumulative, cooperative venture, even for those who won't admit it."

"For the pure in heart," Van Cott said.

"Aw, shut up!" someone shouted.

Van Cott sounded dedicated and independent. A part of me liked him, despite the blind spots.

"The place for extreme individual visions is in literature and art," Turnbull said.

Turnbull did seem a bit prissy. Wear a smile and have friends; scowl and have wrinkles. But people wanted to get along out here; cooperation had been absolutely necessary to build and operate worlds from scratch. Traditions were newer out here. You could be more of a wolf among sheep on Earth, but even there it was getting harder. As for the part about science, it seemed to me that it got done any way it could, cooperation and good manners aside.

The session left me wondering a bit about what kind of person I was. As we stood up to leave, the auburn-haired girl turned around and looked at me with large brown eyes. She smiled, as if commenting on what had been said, then walked away.

Lunch was in Cole Hall, a few hundred yards from our dorm. Most everyone had gone ahead by the time Morey and I came outside. It was still strange, seeing no horizon and the land curving gently upward, over-head, beyond the wispy clouds.

"That Van Cott character, what did you think of him?" I asked.

"I kind of liked him," Morey replied.

"Why?"

"He'll work harder, do more."

"But he's no smarter than us, just wound up more inside."

"Guys like him get the prizes, because they won't let anything distract them."

"Not always," I said loudly. What Morey was saying was true but not likeable, I thought as the large transparent doors slid open and we went inside and got on line. Morey was more like Van Cott. We waited in silence

70

as the long line moved up the ramp from the lounge, and I remembered Marisa telling me that I was not like Morey. Then what was I like? Somebody who worried a lot about himself, she would have said.

The second-floor dining area was all windows, bright with daylight, and the land was all around us, in place of sky.

I scanned the tables. Linda was sitting with Van Cott at the far end. She seemed younger today. I stared, but she was too far away to notice.

"Come on," Morey said impatiently, and we went in to get our food. I didn't like the tone of his voice. I knew that he would consider Linda a distraction, and seeing her with Van Cott had irritated him. As far as I was concerned, Van Cott could use all the distractions he could get.

We walked around the campus after lunch. It was easy to picture where everything was, because the student center and dorms were all within the inner circle of the university. Head outward from the center to get to classes; move toward the outer circle to get to labs. Walks cut across the greens between the rings. These were actually small parks, with benches and play areas for children, tennis courts, and pools.

The student center was a huge three-floor oval with a ribbon of window circling each floor. Morey and I walked into the giant lounge area. A giant holo image stood in the center of the polished red floor, offering newscasts from Earth.

Students sprawled on the floor, walked through the three-dee picture, sat in chairs and hassocks, and leaned against the walls. Multicolored sheen shorts and collarless shirts were everywhere. Haircuts were close among the boys, longer and curly among the girls.

Morey and I didn't fit, with our collared shirts, creased slacks, and longer hair.

"News," I said, crossing my arms and trying to look as if we had come here for that.

"A quake on Mercury," said a woman's giant face, "has taken three more lives among the miners. But the production of metals is not likely to be affected, Earth Authority has announced in New York. There was no public statement from the Mercury community."

Boos and hisses exploded among the students. I felt a wave of sympathy for the dead miners. How could this still be going on? People were dying, and yet there seemed to be no urgency in doing anything about it. I looked at Morey, but he shrugged.

"The Soviet Republics," the reporter continued, "have again claimed to be able to stalemate the Western Alliance's space cyber-force, but the Far Eastern Alliance claims that this is just another bluff, despite the fact that China has given up six disputed border zones in the last six months without one return threat claim. The UN Sec-General describes the affair as just another routine probe in the give and take of peaceful *process politik,* and not a prelude to the return of armed conflict. If the Soviets had a real check threat on Western Alliance peacekeeping forces, he says, then the call committees would already be meeting to determine the move's technical credibility with a view to reaching a new accommodation of gains and concessions. But no such meeting has been asked for by either side in over a decade. . . ."

Most of the students were paying no attention to this part. Morey and I headed for the snack bar.

"What do you think?" I asked. "Is anyone hiding anything?"

"Who cares? I don't have time for politics." We walked through an arch and found a table near the window.

"What do you think would happen if someone were to threaten Earth directly instead of just off-planet forces?"

"Can't happen."

"Why not?"

"Because the panic of even a war scare would hurt business more than real wars have done in the past. Even if someone wiped out some bloc's space-borne force, the result would still be some accommodation. No one wants to attack Earth directly. Couldn't even if they wanted to. The beam weapons are nearly perfect. War has been impractical for some time now, but no one wants to admit it. So they go through the moves, but it's just a way of making agreements. That's why I don't care. It's a waste of time."

He stood up just as I was about to bring up the Mercury situation again.

"What do you want?" he asked. "I'll get it."

"Tall carob shake," I said, realizing that he wasn't going to give me a chance to bring it up just then.

He went to get on line, and I tried to seem as if I'd been sitting there since the year one. It was all unreal, I thought as I gazed out the tall band of windows at the sunsplashed greenery, my feet set firmly against the spinning world that humankind had set in motion out here in the blackness. We had enclosed a bit of space and filled it with dreams; but close in around the Sun, on little Mercury, people were still suffering, paying the price of providing the rest of us with raw materials to keep the dreams running. . . .

"Over there, center of the room," Morey said as he put the shakes on the table and sat down.

I looked and saw Kik ten Eyck sitting with Jake LeStrange.

"I don't think they like us," I said.

Morey shrugged. "Who cares? Not my problem. I'm here to become a physicist."

I was still unsure about wanting to do the same, not if it meant I had to close my eyes to everything else.

We chugged our shakes and pushed the cartons into the drop at the center of the table. I glanced at Jake. He was watching me, so I nodded to him. He smiled and wiggled his fingers at me. I looked at Kik and got a blank stare.

"I'm going for a walk," I said, standing up.

"Want company?"

"Not really," I said without thinking.

He looked at me and I felt that he didn't care; he knew what he wanted and nothing else mattered.

"See you later," he said as I walked away.

I felt restless.

At first I wandered back along the walk to the dorm, but then I cut across the grass; any direction would do.

The air was sweet, with a touch of ozone, as if there had been a storm. Everywhere the greenery showed the skilled hand of a gardener. Even wooded areas were given so much land and no more.

I went around the dorm, climbed over the guard rail, and started down the hill toward the gym. My mind seemed blank, refusing to think about anything; seeing, breathing, and feeling would be enough. My shoes glistened from the moisture in the thick, tall grass, and I wondered about humidity adjustments inside Bernal One. Later I learned that they could make it rain or snow, just for fun.

It was a small world in some ways. No New York City crowds, more like a town. I had already seen some faces more than once.

But to the eye Bernal One was spacious. A sphere of 5 kilometers radius has an inner surface of 314 square kilometers, and a volume of nearly 523 cubic kilometers. I would have to walk 31 kilometers to circle the world at the equator. A population of fifty thousand was small in comparison with Earth's urban areas. New York City is about a thousand square kilometers, Los Angeles thirteen hundred, but both have inhabitants by the millions.

The sunlight was warm on my face as I stared up at the landscape in the sky. Suddenly I tripped and rolled down the hill, tumbling a bit slower than I would have on Earth, because Bernal's rotation produces less than one gravity. I grabbed at the tall grass and stopped myself.

I felt a vibration in my feet as I got up, then the sound of escaping air. A piece of hillside lifted up ahead of me. The ground cracked and clumps of grassy dirt flew into the air as a large hatch opened on power hinges.

I approached slowly and looked into the opening. Blue-white light flickered in the darkness below; a man was climbing up a ladder. I stepped back as his head cleared the rim.

"Hello there, son," he said in a piping voice, and smiled as he climbed out. I saw a stocky, graying man in green coveralls. "Didn't think this lock was still operational," he said, looking around with youthful, blue eyes. "Faulty memory."

"What are you doing?" I asked.

"Routine maintenance checks."

"Where does it lead?"

"Everywhere—on the engineering level." He looked around at the dislodged dirt. "Strange—this lock shouldn't have been covered up." He squinted at me, as if I would know something about it.

"I'm Joe Sorby, from the dorm up there."

"Bernie." He put out his and and I shook it. "Bernie J. Kristol," he added. "At my age you grow into your first name. The rest feels left over from another time. I was just under your dorm, checking the water feeds."

"How long have you been on Bernal?"

He smiled. "I was here when the place was bare, before they put in the land and greenery. The lake was a big hole, the river a muddy ditch." I pictured what he was saying, and a great sense of excitement went through me. "They said we were crazy to build a habitat so big."

"Why did they think that?"

"Accidents, maintenance problems. More people are in danger if something goes wrong. But it's still the biggest and going strong. Where you from?"

"New York City."

"I have a son and grandson there. My house is over

in North Low-G. Those of us who built Bernal got a chance to stay. They still seem to need me, even though I've trained quite a few replacements." He shook his head and chuckled. "Only trouble is they assign my trainees elsewhere as soon as I get them ready."

"You must do a good job." I found myself liking him a lot.

"You know what's what when you train with me on the service level," he boasted, but it didn't bother me. He was obviously telling the exact truth.

"How many people work with you?"

"Oh, maybe a few hundred. But when they get stuck on some problem, it's easier to call me than to work it out from scratch."

"Is it everywhere under the surface, the service level?"

"Come to my office and I'll arrange a tour. Need a job?"

"I don't think so, but I'll take a tour."

"Fine." He was looking at me closely, as if I were a special person. "Well, I have to go. Take care of yourself."

He climbed down into the opening. I guessed that he had to be at least seventy to have been here when Bernal was being built, but I couldn't imagine him slowing up until he was at least a hundred.

The round hatch jerked on its hinges and closed with

a hiss, leaving a shiny cover where the grass had grown. I imagined Bernie's stocky shape loping through the tunnels, his face blasted by flickering blue light as he moved through a world of water pumps, power conduits, air shafts, and waste pipes, which functioned invisibly between the inner garden and the vacuum of space.

I was looking forward to seeing it.

After a moment I noticed movement on the gym field below. A group of young women in shorts were shooting arrows at targets on the gym wall, and it occurred to me that Bernal's spin should create a coriolis effect, curving the paths of the arrows slightly right or left. Coriolis acceleration is the variation in speed as you move inward or outward from the axis of a rotating object. Hurricanes swirl eastward in Earth's northern hemisphere, westward in the southern; tubs drain in a right-handed swirl in the north, left-handed in the south. I recalled the graffiti about peeing on Bernal that I had seen on the shuttle, but I could see no curves in the flight of the arrows. Bernal was too big, its rotation too slow to create a noticeable coriolis effect.

I came down to the last guardrail, where I sat down with my arms around my knees and gazed out into the magnificent space over the gym field. Unsureness crept into me again, and the future became shadowy. I was here to become a physicist and dig out the secrets of the universe. Sure, I was interested in digging out the secrets of nature, but I wasn't sure that I would enjoy the work. It was fun to think about, but I knew enough to know that it would be *work*. It was not going to be work for Morey; he was in love with every bit of it, and ready to put off everything to get where he was going. I knew that I probably couldn't spend the rest of my life in that way, or keep the world away. Physics was not going to be it for me, even though I could do it. Somewhere there was something else, but I couldn't see it clearly yet. I would eventually, because that way lay the truth about myself.

In the meantime I would have to go through school and get what I could out of it; and maybe it would all come to me one day soon, when that small part of me that was stubborn, and smarter than the rest, decided to speak up. It was depressing, but there was nothing else I could do, even though the answers were probably right in front of me.

The archers retrieved their arrows and started over. After the fourth time they collected their shafts and went into the gym. I stared at the empty field. Then I noticed that someone was waving something orange at me, a scarf or a light jacket.

I jumped up and waved back. The figure seemed to glide across the field. She reached the bottom of the hill and started up. I took a deep breath and my pulse quickened as I noticed her red braids.

"Hello," she said, stepping over the rail.

"You were waving at me."

She smiled. "I wasn't."

"What were you doing then?" I demanded.

"Just twirling my jacket." She looked puzzled. "Who knew you were watching?"

"You came when I waved," I continued stupidly, staring at her skimpy white shorts.

"I always walk this way," she replied, ignoring my gaze.

"Well, sorry I waved back, I guess."

She gave me a careful look. "That's okay. What's your name?"

"Joe Sorby." She would remember me at any moment.

"I'm Linda ten Eyck."

As I looked into her wide, green eyes, I saw that she was probably my age, certainly not as old as she had acted when I had arrived. It had been her confidence, the way she had done her job.

"Oh—I was your guide when you came in from Earth." She gave me a knowing, mischievous smile.

I nodded, feeling silly.

"Well, nice seeing you . . . again," she said after a silence.

She brushed her lips lightly with her tongue, slipped past me, and continued up the hill. I stared, noting how beautifully her strong thigh muscles flexed as she climbed.

She didn't look back even once.

I went back to the room and punched up the titles of

81

my course books on the desk screen. Retrieval codes popped up and I slipped them into memory. I was all set to display texts for study. My credit was clear and all my fees had been paid. Three years later: one shiny new physicist.

Maybe Morey was right. Concentrate on one thing and get it done, whatever it takes; catch up on life later. But just then it seemed the hardest thing in the universe to do.

7 Linda

It was the Friday night before the first week of classes. I was sampling course books at my desk, still determined to make a go of it, and finding nothing that would call for memory boosters.

I blanked the screen, sat back, and gazed out the window at the nightglow of the Sun rings as I thought about Linda. Most students were at dorm parties, mixing and pairing, roaming the campus, invading the nearby town or hiking in the woods. The drop in gravity toward the poles was a great novelty among hikers; some couldn't get enough of it.

But the hurried atmosphere of orientation week had turned me off. I didn't like lists of things you were supposed to do, so I had kept pretty much to myself, getting up the determination to start school. Morey and I usually had lunch together, but we were apart the rest of the time.

I was about to close the drapes when Morey came in and sat down on his bed, looking exasperated.

"They think they're here to have a good time!"

"Well, it is the last weekend before classes," I said, turning my chair to face him. "Besides, what do we care?"

"Have you *seen* some of our classmates? They've brought their talking pets. They debate the points of their expensive wristphones. They brag about how many of their relatives have artificial hearts and when they're going to switch to the natural-grown ones, or how many grandparents are in cold storage waiting to be cured of incurable diseases!"

I didn't care much for bioengineered pets either; they were so pathetic mouthing words they couldn't understand, just to please their owners. I had to admit that the showiness of my fellow earthies irked me.

"I thought we'd leave high school crap behind," Morey added.

"Well, the local students seem serious."

"How can you tell?"

"The Mercury situation, for one thing. There's a big demonstration planned."

"That?" He looked at me with contempt. "You think that shows seriousness? Politics. It'll be settled one way or another, but not by us. I don't have the time, and you won't either."

I saw my chance. "See—you do share something with our classmates from Earth. They don't care either."

"Come on! That's a cheap shot."

"People are dying. . . ."

"What do you want?" he demanded angrily. "Do you know what's going to happen? Those who can't make it in school are going to fool themselves into believing they're changing things, or they're going to chase each other in mad affairs. Either way, they won't get their degrees or develop the push that gets the prizes."

"Why get excited, then? Less competition for you."

He looked at me as if I'd betrayed him.

"Calm down," I said. "Things will settle when classes start."

He got up and left the room.

I let out a deep breath as the door slid shut. Then I looked around the room as if in a trance. Morey made me feel that I would never grow up. Maybe no one ever did, and all the adults were faking it; and Morey was faking the nonexistent wisdom of old age. He had done it all through high school. I knew his feelings about politics, and that he held his views honestly. I understood what he meant, but the way he applied it to the Mercury situation rubbed me the wrong way. I couldn't shake the suspicion that Morey really wanted to be Christopher Van Cott.

I punched up 1088.

Linda's face appeared on the screen. "Oh, hello," she said, surprised. To me it sounded as if she had said, "O hollow," which showed what kind of state I was in. Morey and I had often disagreed, but it had always been friendly. Linda's smile was a welcome relief.

"Say," I croaked, "like would go out?"

"What?"

I cleared my throat. "Would you like to go out?"

"Oh." I thought she was going to laugh at me.

"Would you go out this evening, with me?" I managed to say.

She stared at me for a moment. "Say, how tall are you?"

"Uh, about a hundred and seventy-five centimeters. Do you want to or not?"

"I'll meet you in the courtyard of your dorm."

She smiled and blanked the screen.

The night was a bright lunar twilight with a million stars scattered across the blue-green inner surface. The polar Sun rings were a soft blue-white. I stepped closer to the rock garden in the courtyard and read that the minerals and sand were all from the Moon. Then I gazed upward, picking out the roads leading in and out of the town on the other side of the world.

"Hello."

I turned around. Linda stood in front of me. "Hi," I said. She was about my height, maybe a half inch taller.

She stepped close to me. I felt her breath on my cheek. "People from Earth grow slower," she said, smiling.

"I hope you weren't busy, when I called, I mean."

"Just about to wash my hair."

I took in a deeper breath. The knots in her braids looked even more complicated than I remembered. She looked delicious, and she seemed to like me. I felt my pulse quicken.

"I was going to take it out," she said. "Would you like it long?"

"Sure."

She smiled again. "Do you like it like this, with the braids piled on top?"

"Sure."

She touched my cheek gently. "You'll say anything. Where do you want to go?"

"How do you know people from Earth grow slower?" I asked feebly.

"Higher gravity to overcome. You know that. Where are we going?"

"How about the movie museum?" I asked, happy at my good luck.

"What's playing?"

"Let's go and see."

"Okay, Sorby, let's go." Her use of my last name surprised me.

She hooked her arm in mine and we marched across the courtyard. I glanced at her, and she smiled as we started on the path to the student center.

"You're making fun of me," I said.

"I call everyone by their last name until I know them better." She gave my arm a squeeze.

We circled the big white cake of the student center. The museum came into view—a one-story circular building tucked away among some pine trees. We came closer and saw what they were showing:

WAR OF THE WORLDS
THE TIME MACHINE

"Old stuff," she said. "Over a hundred years old. Flat screen, messy sound."

"It's probably been cleaned up and three-deed, but we can always ask for something else." I stopped and looked at her. "Were you expecting me to call?"

"Well—"

I could see that she was tempted to lie about it. "No, Joe," she said finally, "honestly, I wasn't."

Maybe someone else had stood her up. She was at least using my first name now.

"But I wanted you to call," she added, startling me.

"What would you really like to see?" I asked, recovering.

She put a finger to her temple and closed her eyes in mock concentration. Her tight-fitting tan denim suit revealed that she was small breasted and thin, but her small waist made her hips seem rounder.

"Maybe if they have a Bergman," she said, opening her slightly tilted eyes wide. "Got a good look?"

"What?"

She laughed and I swallowed hard. "You've probably seen every film they have," I said.

She hooked her arm in mine again. "Let's go for a walk instead." I felt her warmth and wanted to put my arm around her. I had not gone out since breaking up with Marisa. It seemed very long ago, and I was a bit nervous as well as excited.

"Do you have brothers or sisters?" she asked.

"There's just me."

"Not even one?" She made me feel that I should have double-checked, just to be sure.

"Families are smaller on Earth." I looked up, and again it seemed strange not to see a sky. I kept seeing all the lights as stars. "Where can you see the stars?" I asked. "I mean directly."

"Why? We'd have to wear safety suits on the maintenance level, and the view would be spinning anyway. Let's go to your room. I'll show you how to punch up views from the observatory."

"I know how to do that," I said, missing the point that she wanted to be alone with me.

"You've *seen* stars," she said.

"Not the way I'd like to—outside, in a spacesuit," I replied, turning us down the path to my dorm. "Do you have any large birds here?" I asked.

"Sure—ducks and geese."

"What happens when they fly into the center?"

"Well, they *don't* get stuck. They sort of swim out."

I laughed, feeling that she was interested in me but didn't know what to make of me. I knew I was being moody, picking up on things late. Morey had upset me more than I had realized.

The ceiling flowed with light as we entered the room.

"Here, Joe, look at this," Linda said, sitting down at my desk.

I leaned over her shoulder. "There's the twenty-kilometer O'Neill colony cylinder," she said, touching the screen, "and assorted factories nearby." The view changed, but remained within the L-5 area of space. "Here's the asteroid hollow." It looked like a giant po-tato, cratered and ridged, but was growing green on the inside of the hollow rock, as natural as planting flowers in clay pots.

"I'd like to visit that one," I said.

"They're pretty stuck up over there. Many of the peo-ple are the original asteroid miners who brought the rock into L-5, and they've never gotten over slapping each other on the back about it."

"Well—why not? The Asteroid Belt is a long way from here. You sound like someone from Earth."

"*We* have a right to be critical of ourselves. It's been over twenty years since the hollow was brought in, and many of us feel it wasn't all that necessary, since we can build anything we want out here, without using old rocks."

"I read that the metals mined to make the hollow gave Earth quite a boost at the time."

"Right—Earth, not us. We still had to get our materials from the Moon. It slowed up development of L-5 for a decade, but it made us more self-reliant. Sure, we have a lot of rivalry among ourselves, but it's friendly."

"Tell me about the bad feelings toward Earth."

She turned around and looked at me. "I guess you really *do* want to ruin our evening."

I retreated and sat down on my bed. "Sorry."

"I've never met anyone from Earth," she went on, "who really understood. Don't they teach you anything there? Look—Earth gets everything from us. Power, minerals, drugs, manufactured products of all kinds. Power for the lofting lasers at the spaceports comes from our orbital Sun rigs, and so will the increased power loads for the new gravity catapults. We handle all communications throughout the solar system. Believe me, the antigrav corridors from Earth will use a lot of power—"

"But who would want to deny all this?" I said, feeling a bit defensive.

"Don't you see?" she said. "A political struggle has been going on for some time. Power is shifting to the Sunspacers."

"Well, it happens," I said, "but we're all the same humanity. We come from the solar system."

She shook her head. "Eventually, that's the way it will be. But in the meantime multinational companies are dying. Politicians are losing their bases of power and influence. No one minds the world being richer and people living better. It's the loss of power that hurts most. Whole worlds are being built out here that don't owe to Earthside politicians."

I shrugged. "More adaptable leaders will win out. It'll even out." I was sounding a bit like Morey, and I didn't like it.

"Right. Earth won't really suffer economic hardship. It's what happens in the transition that's worrying many of us."

"What do you mean?"

"The people who came out here worked hard, Joe. They built the industrial centers on Luna, Mercury, Mars, and the Asteroids. But they didn't have any real say about their lives until they had something to bargain with, in the form of deliverable energy and resources. Then the politicians lined up for power positions in Earth Authority, which gave them their base for local national power. And then it occurred to the home world that it wouldn't do to let the various Sunspace Settlements get too self-sufficient. Big decisions are still made by Earth Authority, no matter how many representatives from Sunspace sit in."

"But from what I know, the Mercury situation is the only real complaint . . . "

"That's enough! Do you know what's going on out there?"

"Well, I've heard it's bad. . . ."

She was quiet suddenly.

"I'm very interested, Linda."

She smiled. "Sorry to shout. You're right, the Sunspace Settlers are doing very well—so well that Earth is recognizing their importance. But that's what makes the Mercury problem so intolerable, by comparison."

"Were you born here?" I asked.

"No, but I grew up here. My parents brought my brother and me from New Zealand when we were babies. Both our parents died in a shuttle accident when we were in high school."

"I'm sorry," I said, feeling inadequate.

Linda was looking at the floor. "Kik dropped out of school and apprenticed himself so we could stay, but I think he wanted to leave school and work in a trade anyway. We're on our own now, so he could go back, but I think he's one of those people who can't appreciate it until they're older."

I wondered if I was the same.

"We're different," she continued, "but we're very close. He looked out for me. I hope I get a chance to help him someday."

"What are you studying?" I asked, trying not to think about myself.

"Economics and metallurgy. Materials synthesis in general. I want to help make decisions out here one day." She got up and sat down next to me. "Sorry I shouted," she said again, "but I like you, and I can't stand people I like being . . . well, confused."

"I wanted to know."

She leaned against me. I slipped my arm around her slender waist and she looked at me suddenly, her eyes wide, face slightly flushed. We wanted each other, and we both knew it.

We kissed, and I felt the tension between us drain away. Her body seemed soft and firm at the same time.

"Good?" she asked after a while, her warm breath tickling my nose.

"Hmmmmmm," I said, looking forward to the rest of the evening.

"One kiss and your mind crumbles," she whispered, smiling radiantly.

I laughed and she kissed me fiercely.

My phone buzzed.

"Probably my roommate, checking to see if the room

is free." I struggled to the desk and opened the line, but not the picture.

"Hello?" I said.

"Joe? Eva and I are on a conference link," Dad answered after the three-second silence.

I sat down.

"Where's your pic?" Mom asked cheerfully.

"Busted, I guess, but I hear you fine."

"How's it going?" Dad said.

"Good. How are you two doing?" I couldn't think of what else to say. Linda got up and left the room as I waited.

"Have you guests?" Mom asked. "We've disturbed you."

"No—no, I was only studying."

Silence.

"On Friday night?" Dad said. "Has the term started?" He should have known that classes started on Monday.

"Just looking over course books, actually."

As I waited for the silence to pass, it occurred to me that the call had disturbed Linda somehow, that she had not left just to let me talk in private.

"That's very good," Mom said, trying to sound caring. I resented the effort.

"Are you there, son?"

"Yes, Dad, I'm here." I opened the visual and saw their faces on the split screen. They tried to look cheerful as my picture reached them.

"There you are," Dad said. "You look good. No doubts, I see."

"I'm glad," Mom added.

"Tell you what," Dad said. "One or both of us will try to call at least once a week."

"I'll be here." One, two, three.

"Take care," Mom said as the picture faded.

I got up and went to the door, thinking that Linda was waiting outside. I stepped out and looked in both directions, but the hallway was empty.

"Linda," I said loudly, hoping that she had simply gone for a walk around the turn. There was no answer. I went looking for her, but it was obvious after a moment that she had left.

I was angry when I returned to the room, but not at Linda. My parents had called me to say nothing important, and had ruined my evening at the same time. Actually, I was as much puzzled as angry. Was I such bad company that Linda had taken the chance to get away?

8 Classes

I walked around the campus circles that Saturday. My weight dropped slightly as I wandered away from the center line of the equator, but I couldn't really feel the difference until I had gone a ways and come back. I looked at a lot of buildings, tennis courts, and swimming pools. The crystal-clear openness of Bernal's inner space was a wonder that could not be worn out.

Once in a while I saw a sign:

NO CHILDREN PAST POINT C

Only adults were permitted to live in the lower-g regions around the poles. Children needed something close to Earth gravity to grow normally, especially if they ever wanted to return to Earth. Kids were common in the rural toruses, which were outside the sphere and free of changes in gravity. Child monitors routinely returned children who escaped into low-g zones.

The campus seemed deserted. Everyone was resting up from the partying of the night before and getting ready for tonight's socializing. I sympathized with Morey and wished that it were Monday, even though I knew that for most students it was just a way of building up motivation for schoolwork. Morey didn't need it, apparently, and I was in no mood, after Linda, to start something that might distract me from my resolve to give college a long, hard shot.

I sat around in the student-center lounge, listening to more about Mercury on the news holos. A strike by the miners would cut off the flow of metals into Earth's industrial space, with serious consequences for the quality of life on Earth itself. The commentator also claimed that the Near Earth Space Habitats would also suffer to some degree, but I wondered if this was an attempt to shift the sympathies of a portion of the Sunspacers away from Mercury's mining community. It was true that Bernal and the other habitats needed rare metals and structural components to keep up their maintenance, but I couldn't believe that shortages would be life threatening. Another commentator pointed out that the habitats were well stocked with maintenance supplies. The profits of many companies would drop, however. No one really thought that would be a good thing, but the Sunspacers were willing to sacrifice to help their sister community.

I got up after a while and walked back toward the

dorm, wondering about Linda. I wanted to call her, but why should I put her on the spot? If she wanted to see me again, she would call and explain why she had disappeared, or she would ignore me. I couldn't believe that she had been faking her attraction for me. There had to be other reasons. I would have to wait and see.

The small amphitheater was crowded on Monday morning. I found an aisle seat in the back row.

The room quieted at 9:01. My empty stomach rumbled gently, and I wondered if it was going to detect coriolis acceleration after all.

"I'm Gordon Vidich," the Physics 1 professor said in a rich bass. He was middle-sized, black hair combed straight back, looking like glossy paint from where I sat. "Most of you are preparing for a science career. How many physicists?" Half the hands shot up, most of them belonging to women. I figured I could become a physicist even if I didn't raise my hand. "A few pet peeves," he continued. "I know that you're in love with the mystery of the universe, with what's out there as well as with the bit of you that's curious about it. Existence *is* ultimately mysterious, but we *do* know a lot short of final answers. Speculate, but *please* show me *always* that you know the difference between the assemblage of facts we call a theory and speculations that may or may not contain a few sparse facts. I want to see in you a *habit of*

SUNSPACER

mind that will always pit theory and speculation against *some* kind of experimental experience." I pictured him peeling off his thin layer of black hair and tossing it to the class as his concluding point. "If the experiment can't be done," he continued, "wait until it can. Don't build careers on its *imagined* income." No one laughed at his bad substitution of income for outcome. "We had a lot of imaginary science at the turn of the century, until the public couldn't tell crackpots and popularizers from honest scientists. Anyone might *guess* the nature of the universe, or even the outcome of an experiment. The number of answers is always limited. But that does no good unless a mathematically expressed experiment pulls your answer out of the realm of possible worlds into our own." He seemed to be trying to look up at his bushy eyebrows. "Clear?"

Heads nodded.

"You must go on your knees," he shouted, "before the universe of facts, as you weave them into theories!"

I tingled from the projected energy of his spoon-feeding.

"Give your name when you speak," he followed up softly. "If I forget, it will be because you have failed to say anything interesting."

Uneasy laughter.

"Tell me the difference between gravity and centrifugal force."

"Christopher Van Cott," a voice said from the front row. "Gravity's a *field*, like magnetism. Centrifugal force is a product of acceleration."

Vidich shrugged. "Vague terms, field and force. Why *should* there be a difference at all?"

An auburn-haired girl stood up in the third row, the same one who had gotten the better of Van Cott at orientation. "Rosalie Allport. The more general a question, the less likely it can be answered in a scientific theory. *Why* is a question that may or may not one day be answered, depending on how specific a chain of lesser answers we can construct."

"Good!"

Van Cott snorted.

Vidich glared at him. "That's all for now. I wouldn't want any of you to miss the beautiful day outside."

It took a moment for the class to laugh.

Chemistry 1 started at 10:15.

Tall, big boned, and blond, Helga Akhmatova spoke in British tones as she glided back and forth, very relaxed in a loose tweed coverall.

"Chemistry's link to other sciences," she said, "its sharing of problems, has only increased with time. Physics is fundamental, of course, followed by chemistry and biology. Then we gaze across a great abyss to psychology and the social sciences. Crude divisions, admittedly, and the abyss is not all that empty. But if you can imagine a bridge of special, connecting areas, then you can get a feeling for how a complex universe, with things like persons and nations, is built up, layer by layer, out of fundamentals which themselves do not have the properties to be found at higher levels. Chemistry is one of the first hierarchies of complexity in the slow climb toward a unified science of nature." She paused and smiled. "I suggest that you grasp problems as you can and work from there to other things, going back only when you must. Don't be afraid of gaps. Fill them in or learn to live with them." She smiled again. "You will all do well enough, I expect."

She made me believe every word. I realized, with some uneasiness, that what she had said applied also to self-knowledge. What was the use, then, if we could never know ourselves completely?

Morey and I sat together in Astronomies, which began at 11:10.

"I'm Muhammad Azap," the tall, slightly plump professor said, closing his mouth as if to trap the p. He scratched his fine brown hair. "I'll assume that nothing escapes you. Wing it if you wish. Maybe something interesting has got your attention. Who knows? As long as you remedy weaknesses before term's end." He was spooky, but I liked him.

He turned sideways, as if trying to disappear. "Eight

different astronomies from now until May, from visual to gravity-lens observations. What's the difference between astronomy last century and now? Don't say there are more kinds of astronomy, or that you have to know more physics."

"It's become more of an experimental science," Rosalie Allport said softly, "as we've moved out into Sunspace."

Azap nodded. "Astronomy will become a completely experimental science when human beings and their instruments can go anywhere in the known universe." He looked at us as if he had delivered himself of a great truth. "Tomorrow the hard stuff. Go to lunch."

Morey shook his head as we stood up. "A loon, but I like him."

"He must be good to be here," I said.

Linda came up the aisle with Jake LeStrange. I tensed, but they didn't notice me. Then Rosalie Allport came by, and I had a chance to see more than her back for a change. Her hair was tied in a short ponytail. She had clear brown eyes and full but delicate lips. I stared. She smiled and looked away.

"Come on, let's go," Morey said, nudging me a bit too hard.

I turned and looked at him. He smiled. "I can see how you're going to waste your time."

*   *   *

Human Development A, at 1:10, sounded like a course to housebreak scientific types, to give them culture and couth, as Morey put it.

We sat down four rows from the pit. Van Cott turned around in front of me.

"Say, Morey, don't you think we could get this stuff on our own?"

"Probably."

So they had met, I thought as a smiling, middle-sized man with white hair walked into the pit. He wore an all-in-one black slacks/white shirt combo with green bow tie.

"A clown," Morey whispered.

"Good afternoon. My name's Christian Praeger. This is probably the only course you'll take whose subject matter is beyond all of us. I'm not always sure myself what the subject matter is, but it has to do with making some sense of what humankind has done in its short history."

Van Cott was shifting restlessly in his seat.

Praeger smiled. "Does human history make a pattern of some kind? Is there a vision which unifies human knowledge? Einstein once said that he wouldn't try politics because it was much harder than physics—too many variables, and calling for decisions, not just understanding, where too little was known, at moments when decisions still had to be made, and where partial success was the best that could be expected.

"There will be a lot of necessary nonsense in this course, but we'll try to remove it by developing some kind of crap detector. There's no *one* way to make one, but it does demand the readiness to shift perspective while retaining a sense of values."

"Whatever that means," Van Cott whispered. I didn't like admitting that he had a point.

"As scientists," Praeger continued, "each of you must be able to share in the general culture, if for no other reason than that it is the culture that supports science. I know the dedication required to make a success of a career in science, to even get to the point where one has a *chance* at making *a* contribution, much less something major."

"I wish he could talk," Van Cott said.

"It's still us against them," Morey added.

"But the investment of time and patience also belongs to the burden of an artist or writer. I remember what it took for me to get degrees in physics and chemistry."

"No kidding," Van Cott whispered in surprise. "He has scientific degrees?"

"We'll be reading the so-called great books. There are only a few hundred of these. Read casually this term, but you'll find that your care will grow as our discussions become more pointed. Your interest will increase and you'll be pleased to work harder. Many past students have told me that this work complemented their scien-

S   U   N   S   P   A   C   E   R

tific careers, putting their later work in a much-needed human context. I hope that you will come to feel the same."

"We're in church," Van Cott said softly.

"Quiet," I said, nudging him.

"Human cultures have advanced on more than one front at a time—science is one of the most successful, and the one that sets the most exacting models of honesty and attention to merit. But on other fronts—"

"Example!" Van Cott shouted.

"Well, the habit of complex observation in literature, for one. Human characters are *entered*, social systems *observed*, with a personal accuracy that cannot be accomplished in other ways. An analog of experience remains that is often truer than formal histories, of how people felt about themselves and the universe. Then there's music, a realm of striving forms, pure feeling and beauty, atmosphere, rationally expressed, voicing the ineffable. . . ."

I was moved by Praeger's love of his subject.

"Sounds good," Van Cott said loudly.

"How many of you have read Milton?" Praeger asked.

Van Cott laughed. "You mean that clumsy poem where all the science is wrong?"

"Can someone else answer?"

I raised my hand and stood up. "It seemed very real to me."

106

"Exactly the point. The cosmology of *Paradise Lost*, or Dante's *Inferno*, was the real stuff for many people, once."

"Astrology!" Van Cott shouted.

"It was a way of dealing with human fears and hopes."

"So is hiding under the bed," Van Cott added.

"I see it's going to be an interesting semester," Praeger said, completely undisturbed.

Van Cott was a go-getter; that was why Morey liked him. Dedicated as Morey was, he needed to see others swimming in the same direction. I had nothing against dedication, but Van Cott was shouting his to the world. I didn't like his style, even if he was brilliant; but that made me feel backward, even primitive, to notice his style and not his substance. I think Morey needed to see me swimming his way, but I felt that maybe I had nothing to crow about. If I did, then maybe I'd be snickering along with the two of them and having a fine time of it.

As the lecture hall began to empty, Van Cott turned to me and grinned. "That was pretty good, Sorby." For a moment I thought he was making fun of me, but then I saw that he meant it. In his own way Van Cott was sincere.

And then I didn't know what to think.

Sunlight from the rings was warm on my face as I lay in the grass on the hillside. I thought of all the course work, but I didn't see myself doing it, even though the first day of classes had filled me with visions of new worlds to know.

I sat up and looked around. This bit of ground near Bernie's lock would make a great reading spot. I lay back again and closed my eyes. The Sun was very special here, tamed and turned inward by the mirrors of human dreams made real. The past seemed like a bad dream, the future too far away to even think about.

I liked my teachers; they made me feel that I could accomplish everything. I felt happier, just lying there, than I had ever felt before in my life, even though part of me knew that I had to be kidding myself. I didn't want to admit that what I could do fairly well was probably not what I wanted to do at all—but what was there for me to do? How can you be happy when you suspect that you no longer know what you want, and refuse to face up to the problem? I wanted to be here, to be part of the Sunspace way of life. School, I realized dimly, had only been my way of getting out here.

9 Rosalie

I felt great for about six weeks.

Fantastic classes.

Discussions spilling over into the snack bar, to dinner and late into evenings. I felt I really belonged.

Individual arguments with professors and tutors.

Akhmatova, Azap, Praeger, and Vidich loaded us with ammunition, and we fired it at each other without mercy. They fought us tooth and brain, yet managed to stay on our side. I had no time to think about myself.

There weren't the jokers and class clowns of high school, or the troublemakers who would get suspended. Even obnoxious Van Cott seemed more human and it didn't seem to matter what I thought of him.

For a while Morey and I became friendly with two students down the hall, David Kihiyu and Marco Pellegrini. We often ate together, and sometimes studied with them and Marco's girlfriend, Narita Sykes. But I soon noticed how much like Morey they were, and that reminded me that I was pretending to fit in, so I could get through school as I had decided. David and Marco wanted to know everything. David would sometimes wake us up in the middle of the night to tell us about an idea he'd dreamed, and Morey would listen while I drifted off. Narita was more like Van Cott. I was sure she and Marco talked physics in bed. I knew dedication when I saw it, and I felt bad that I didn't have it; but it was easy, at first, to ignore my feelings.

The days were exciting, intense, and tiring, especially when you were forced to listen to technical talk in the showers. We took a field trip to the Research Shacks near the outer edge of L-5's volume of space, where they did the dangerous work with dense states of matter, the control of inertia, and the further applications of negative-g, which still couldn't do more than hurl a ship off-planet; but one day negative-g would push a ship directly, as part of its drive, and take us out to the stars. Doing that was a more exciting idea, for me, than understanding the physics that would make it possible.

The Shacks looked like a collection of giant tin cans as our shuttle pulled away. I felt a thrill at knowing what was being done there.

It was a short hop back to Bernal, but the Moon was as far away as Earth. As seniors we would visit the big labs on Lunar Farside; some of us would even work there one day, the recruiters had assured us.

As I gazed at Luna's dry, silvery face, I felt the vast emptiness of space, the smallness of worlds where life had fought to establish itself, and I remembered that I was still a problem to myself.

"You're not very serious about physics," Morey said to me on the last evening in August. David and Marco had just left. We were at our desks, entering the day's work.

I stopped and stared at him.

"Come on, Joe, you just don't have the way of talking. You don't go after things."

"You mean I'm not Van Cott," I said nervously.

"I'm your friend and should tell you."

"Well you're wrong."

"I hope."

"What do you mean?"

"You're always running off somewhere."

"So?"

"You're not doing *enough* work."

"My grades are as good as yours!"

He clenched his teeth and smiled. "You know that doesn't mean much by itself." He had lost some weight, making him look less bearlike, taller. "You're *knocking* off the work quite well, even expertly, but you're not digging into it, living it the way David does, or Narita. You're not letting it take you over, the way it should if you're going to do original work."

"I keep it to myself," I muttered, feeling a bit guilty.

He shook his head. "No, it would show. A whole new world should be growing inside you. Not just the thrills of it, but the hard, close thinking. It may sound pompous to you, but there's no other way to say it."

A part of me knew he was right, but I wasn't going to admit it.

"And you're always talking about engineering. More since we came back from the Shacks."

"What's wrong with that?" I asked, even though I knew what he would say. "Our technology doesn't do half of what our science says is possible."

"But I thought you wanted physics," he said wearily, "to be at the frontiers of science doing basic work."

"Maybe engineering is for me."

He looked shocked. "That's for second stringers, Joe."

"And no friend of yours is *that*," I said.

"Be serious." The light from his screen flickered on his face. "You're not being fair. I thought we could talk to each other."

"Leave me alone, Morey, will you?"

"Can't take it?"

I glared at him.

He grinned.

"You changing to psych?" I asked.

"Maybe—there's a whole universe inside every skull. I didn't realize how big medicine was out here. There's

bio-research going on they wouldn't dare do on Earth."
He was trying to show me that his interests were wider
than I thought.

"Well, I'm not going to be one of your cases," I said,
feeling panicky, as if I should run around and sound
the alarm for a fire or flood; it *was* an emergency, but
I just sat there, staring at the screen.

"I'm sorry," he said, turning off his screen. "Maybe
you're paying too much attention to politics."

I wasn't, but the way he said it made me angry. "You
don't feel anything for the people of Mercury."

"I do, but I can't help."

"You could sign a petition, go to a meeting with me."

"Yeah, maybe, but my studies come first. Not a grade,
my *studies*, if you know the difference." He shook his
head. "It's what I came here for, Joe." He looked straight
at me. "Linda filled your head with Sunspacer politics."

"I saw her only once."

"Sure," he said, leaning back. "She made you feel
guilty."

"There are issues!"

He was silent for a moment. "Okay, but you don't
have to throw away your career for something that'll get
settled anyway."

"I'll get through anyway."

"Stubborn pride isn't enough."

I didn't have to be his kind of physicist, I told myself,

but the truth in what he was saying was getting to me more than I realized.

"Sorry, Joe," he said suddenly. "Maybe I'm wrong."

I swallowed hard and took a deep breath. He was only trying to let me down easy. More than anything, just then, I wished to be without body or feelings—a pure mind knowing everything there was to know, drinking in all the light in the universe. Pure minds don't have friends, I told myself as I looked at Morey's sour expression.

"You're late," Morey whispered in Astronomies the next day. "What's the matter with you?"

I stared ahead tensely, waiting for the hour to go by. Azap ran through the interstellar measurement wars at the turn of the century, when it had seemed that the universe was getting smaller as the yardsticks were revised under the pressure of some very clever criticisms. At the end of the ten-year fracas, the universe got larger again. As if the universe could care much, I thought.

I noticed Linda and Jake in the front row. They seemed to be together again. I had learned that she had gone out with me after their last quarrel. They never stayed apart for long, Narita Sykes had told me that morning in the snack bar. But that still didn't seem like enough to explain why she had run off when my parents had called, I had thought as I listened to Narita impart her wisdom.

"Jake isn't what you think he is," she had said. "He's a brilliant astrophysics student. A bit older than us, but he got a late start. He works to pay for school. His math has appeared in the journals." I didn't like the way she had rolled her eyes.

Morey was in a hurry to leave as the class ended. "Are you coming?"

I motioned for him to go without me. We were being polite to each other, but it wasn't the same. I didn't like the idea that anyone might know more about me than I did.

I saw Rosalie Allport coming up the aisle as the hall emptied. On impulse, I stood up and approached her.

"Hello, I'm Joe Sorby."

She stopped and smiled. "Yes, I know, you're in my other classes also."

"Could we go out sometime? I've wanted to ask."

She grimaced. "There's just no time. I have to study and help out in my father's bookstore in town. Sorry."

"Can I come see you there?"

"I can't stop you, but I'll still be busy."

She went past me, leaving me alone in the empty hall.

I went back to the dorm and sat at my desk, determined to study.

The phone rang.

I opened the line.

"Hello, son," Dad's face said after the delay.

"Oh, hello." The screen flickered.

"You're probably very busy, but I wanted to ask if you're coming home for intersession."

"Sure!" Suddenly I wanted to escape for a little while into my earlier life, where I had not doubted the future, just to get back my sense of direction. Then I saw the pained look on Dad's face. "What's wrong?"

I waited.

"It's just that I'm taking a leave of absence from work. Everything's going into storage and I'm moving out of the apartment. I'm not sure where I'll be, so I called to tell you not to come."

"I'll visit Mom, then." One, two, three.

"Uh, actually she's looking for work herself and won't have time."

"Oh. When will you have a new address?" The thought of never seeing that apartment again made me feel panicky. I was being eased out on my own, and it felt spooky.

"Don't know. I'll be traveling."

"Will you see Mom?"

"I'm sure going to try, son."

My room would no longer be there. "But where will you live when you come back to work?" It would all belong to someone else.

"The institute will find me a smaller place, if that's what I need then."

"I understand," I said softly, my stomach drifting around inside me as the seconds dragged on.

"Can you stay there during the break?"

"Sure, no problem." I wanted to tell him that it would be a big hassle, just to see what he would do.

"You're sure, Joe?"

I nodded.

He looked relieved finally. "I have to remind myself how fast you're growing up and can take care of yourself."

"Don't worry," I said, and waited. He hadn't meant to be cruel, asking me if I planned to come home, just thoughtless maybe. I felt angry and miserable.

"I'd better sign off and let you work."

For what? The past was gone and my future was ready to crumble. I was nowhere.

"So long," I managed to say, waiting for him to hang up.

The screen winked off. My face stared back at me from the shiny surface. I looked away, drained. My bed looked inviting.

I lay down and let the cotton into my brain, hoping that I would collapse into a small black hole and disappear.

The Sun was hot on my back and my arms were tiring as I swam toward the rock. The noise of the crowd on the crescent of white beach behind me was muted by the surf.

Foam washed over the green seaweed clinging to the stone. The girl sat up and looked at me as I stood up awkwardly on the jagged rocks. I climbed up and sat down next to her.

She smiled. Her breasts were full, her hips round over a bright-blue bikini; drops of water and grains of sand shared the tangle of her black hair. I smelled beer on her breath.

She stirred as if from a trance, stood up, and dived into the sea, just missing the sharp rocks. I admired her tanned muscles as she pulled toward shore, her long hair floating behind her.

A stocky man waded in and pulled her free of the breakers. She held his arm as they climbed a high dune.

I cried out to her and opened my eyes to the ceiling.

I'd had the dream a few times after the meeting on the rock, but that had been when I was fourteen; yet here it was again, as haunting and full of loss as ever. Would things have been different with Marisa, or if my parents had been happier? Or would the problems have been the same, but with different details?

I still had half the afternoon, so I hiked across the campus toward town. I stopped midway on the bridge and gazed down into the river. A lonely, faceless shape stared up at me from over a shadow railing.

The river curved down gently from the lake. Ducks

congregated in the shallows, ducking for food. A slight breeze made me shiver. I went across and entered Riverbend.

Three good-sized towns sit inside Bernal. Riverbend is the closest to the university, so named because the stream bends here as it comes out of the lake. Windy is near the south pole; in spite of its name, the air currents there are very mild. Skytown is directly opposite Riverbend across the sphere, so they're actually up in each other's skies. Riverbend is a large circle of comfortably spaced modular buildings, mostly one and two floors. Streets are laid out in tangents, making a pattern of multicolored structures and white-paved ways. Skytown is a big triangle, Windy a square. Riverbend looks like circles and squares within each other.

A trolley passed me as I came off the bridge and walked by the Sunspace Hotel. A few guests were lounging in chairs by the river. I wondered if any of these men and women were part of the delicate negotiations about Mercury, which had just begun at the hotel.

I went by the First Bank of Bernal, a small one-floor box of glass and brick that housed the credit terminals, and continued up Main Street, past the drugstore, a clothes outlet, and a deli. Arthur's Hart, a bar and sandwich shop, stood on the next corner, next to the only bookstore on Bernal.

I whirled through the archaic revolving door and

stopped just inside a giant cube with book-covered walls. There was a catwalk halfway up to the ceiling. Ladders and footstools waited conveniently, but I saw no customers.

I looked up and saw Rosalie coming around the catwalk.

"Are all these books real?" I asked.

She leaned over the rail and smiled. "What are you doing here?"

I shrugged. "Come to see you, I guess."

She frowned and started down the ladder. I watched her, noticing again how pretty she was. She stepped down gracefully and turned to face me. I wanted to kiss her.

She seemed embarrassed by my attention. I looked around at the books.

"Most of them are copies," she said impatiently, "but we can fax any volume in any language ever published."

"Ever?"

"If Earth has copies in memory storage, with a plan of the original binding, or if someone somewhere has an actual copy we can examine. At the beginning, you must have a physical copy to reproduce. Searching out books that were not stored is quite a job."

"I can dial up anything really important on my screen."

She knew I was baiting her, but she remained serious. "A lot of people still want the actual book, especially an exact copy of the original edition, which may no longer

120

exist. You'd be surprised how few books have survived from the last two centuries. We can even reproduce the antique smell of the original volume."

"How's that?"

"We call up the pages, run them on the same kind of paper and bind downstairs, as many as needed. Printing is nothing, the *style* of printing and binding everything. And our copies last forever. No acid yellowing or crumbling of paper."

"You do it by hand?"

"Of course not. But the machines do need programming for accuracy, and that takes a good eye."

"You don't sell many," I said.

"More than you might guess. But they're too much to store, so many people have brought books back when they couldn't keep them. They make good display. We do have steady customers. Some people really hook on collecting, once they realize that they can have almost anything."

"That's dumb. How many times will a book be opened after it's been read? You can always get it again from a memory bank. It's more efficient."

She shrugged. "You don't understand collecting. There's a man in Windy who had us run off a set of Ace Double Science Fiction paperbacks from the middle of the last century. He won't stop until he has all science fiction to 2001."

"Want to have a late lunch?" I asked politely.

She smiled. "I go to Arthur's next door." I was staring into her clear brown eyes. She seemed bustier than I remembered. She was wearing a sheer white blouse and gray slacks. The skin on her neck seemed very soft.

"Well, are we going?" she asked.

Arthur's Hart was empty, except for two older people down at the far end of the bar. We sat down at a corner table.

"Two beers and ham clubs," Rosalie said as the bartender noticed us. "Is that okay, Joe?"

I nodded and she punched in the order on the bright call board in the center of the table. "You like the store?" she asked.

"It's great," I said.

"Dad's hobby, really, but he doesn't get much time from his job as biblioprogrammer at the university, so I try to help. He locates books through the terminal links with Earth. He's always looking for books to redo for his idea of an ultimate library—the most important books from every age. He doesn't think there should be more than about a thousand volumes. He's always weeding and replacing."

"I'd rather read than own books."

The roller brought our food. We removed the plates and it scooted away. I swallowed some beer and took a bite of sandwich.

"Dad once took a trip to Earth to buy a few actual first editions. He says if there's ever a war on Earth, computer memories might be wiped, so there should be physical libraries somewhere, as a hedge."

"We'll never have wars again," I said.

"I'm not so sure."

"Earth is too well off."

"Natural disasters can threaten memory banks. Some physical books will always survive." She glanced at the timer over the bar. "Can we have news?" she called. The bartender nodded.

The wall at the end of the long room grew hazy. A holo of New York appeared.

"My hometown," I said pompously, hating my voice.

"Really?" She smiled.

The caster appeared against the skyline. "Good afternoon. I'm Keith Lamas in New York. With thirty lives lost in the newest quakes on Mercury, the miners have called a strike, cutting off all heavy-metal boosts to Earth Orbit until a date is set for the construction of an orbital habitat around Mercury. The surface of the planet, they claim, is too dangerous for them and their families, and will become even more hazardous if mining operations are expanded in efforts to tap the planet's metal-rich core with nuclear explosives. . . ."

"Couldn't they build their own?" I asked. "They have the energy and resources to build a thousand habitats."

"It's not that easy, Joe." She seemed disappointed by my comment, as if she wanted to like me but I had made it harder. "They don't have the time or the work force of specialists to do it quickly enough, without waiting a decade to move in. The habitat would have been ready by now if Earth had kept its promise back when."

"How many people would it take?"

"To do it quickly—maybe five thousand skilled workers and tons of machinery. I'd volunteer."

"The Asteroid Belt has repeated its support for Mercury's demands," Lamas continued, with a shot of Mercury and the Sun at his back, "even as negotiations have broken down at L-5. The other Sunspace Settlements are expected to follow suit. . . ."

"That's us," Rosalie said.

"Earth won't go to war," I said.

She laughed. "Earth is too dependent." She sipped her beer. "It will have to give in if Mars, Luna, the Asteroids, and the Sunspace Settlements all support Mercury."

I didn't like accepting Earth as the villain, even though it probably deserved it. So I took the other side, just to see what Rosalie would say. "What can they do?" I asked. "Go to war? Everyone would lose."

She touched my hand, as if I were a hopeless dunce. "Joe, the truth is that Earth takes a lot from the rest of the Solar System and doesn't keep its promises. Not because it's entirely mean, but because it's easier. Earth doesn't want to know how people live elsewhere, as long as it doesn't have to tear up its own environment, as long as it gets its metals, electronics, power, from the satellite grid—especially the biotechnology that keeps the old politicians alive. The off-planet death rates are incredible for an age when people can theoretically live forever."

"People die on Earth too," I said feebly. "You can't blame every accident on Earth."

She bit her lower lip and stared at me. "Accidents are one thing. Sunspacers are willing to take risks, but not to throw their lives away!"

I'd never seen people get hurt or die. It bothered me that it was happening somewhere, needlessly, while others gained by it. People on Earth lived decent lives because of what the Sunspacers had accomplished. If the sky frontier had not been opened, Earth might now be living a double life—islands of prosperity would exist in a sea of famine and human die-off. What kind of people would be living on the islands of prosperity? I had grown up believing that such things no longer happened. I'd heard about it, but always with the idea that it was about to be taken care of. But the open wounds were still with us, and I felt my anger getting ready to break out.

"But what can we do about it?" I asked, echoing Morey.

The news was ending:

". . . and the last slugs of refined ores will reach Earth orbit in three months. There will be no more if the miners stop the flow. This is Keith—"

The bartender turned off the holo.

We finished our lunch uneasily.

"What can Bernal do?" I asked.

I could see that she wanted to answer me carefully. "The town councils will support the miners, of course, but we can do much more—refusing to service the powerstat beamers in Near Earth Orbit, for one thing, or to run the ore tugs that guide the slugs coming in from Merk, so even the ore still on the way would be useless to Earth. The thirty communities of L-4 and 5 are a whole country. Space travel would stop without us. Earth would be quarantined. We could seize any ship coming up into Earth Orbit. Earth will give in for the biotechnology alone. Its whole medical system depends on substances manufactured in zero-g. A lot of powerful lives would end, just when they thought they might live forever."

"It would be murderous to cut off a world like that," I said.

"Murderous! Look at Earth's history of killing. Millions of species died out before 2000. A good portion of the planet was returning to desert by then. The planet is still heating up from all the atmospheric pollution. Do you know how many people died of starvation, how

many failed to reach their normal body weight and intelligence for lack of food?"

"You don't like Earth much," I said.

She stared at me without blinking. "That's not the
point, Joe. Earth is still doing it. Those miners have been
asking for a decent place to live for more than twenty
years now."

"I know."

"Keep it down," the bartender said.

"It *was* promised," she continued more softly. "The
Sunspacers saved Earth's ass at the turn of the century—
with energy, the industrial work that couldn't be done
on the planet, with resources and medicines. And do
you know what people still think? That *they* did it, and
that convicts don't deserve better anyway."

"Well, we're all human beings. . . ." I was about to say
from Earth. "So what's holding things up?"

"Our reps are still a minority on Earth, but UN Earth
Authority will approve the Mercury project, no matter
what it costs, or risk a major break between Earth and
off-worlders."

"Didn't sound like it on the news."

"The threat of the strike will push things right. Haven't
you seen the holos of Mercury, the conditions in those
underground hovels? Where have you been?"

"I've seen them. But what can I do personally?"

"Do you really want to know?"

We were silent.

"I know what's right," I said finally, not wanting to seem uncaring.

"Sorry, Joe, I didn't mean to shout."

We got up and walked over to the register, where she punched in her payment. "This is on me," she said.

We came outside. "I've got to get back to the store," she said. Her eyes searched my face for a moment.

"Can I call you sometime?" I asked.

She touched my face gently. "Sure." Then she turned and went into the bookstore.

The river was turning a deeper blue as I walked back across the bridge. I felt that I was exactly what Rosalie had taken me to be—an overprotected kid from Earth, an only child let loose reluctantly by a jealous planet. I tried not to think as I looked around in the fading light, surprised again by my own existence. I was a traveler with no memory, newly arrived in a world where everyone seemed to know more than I did. No wonder I didn't know what I wanted. I was growing up, moving from past to future, so how could I be expected to see ahead? I was still too close to the beginning.

Bernal's inlay of greenery darkened. Lights blinked on in buildings and shot down roadways as I hurried back to the dorm. It seemed that the worlds could solve their problems, if they wanted to; and so would I, once

I decided what was important to me. Adults are degenerated children, Morey liked to say. Spooked by fear and doubt, they lose the imaginative flexibility of their youth and freeze up, hanging on to what they have, unable to decide new things. Was that happening to me, before I'd had a chance to grow up?

The phone rang as I came into the room.

"Joe?" Linda's voice asked as I opened the line. There was no picture.

"Hello, I'm here."

"May I talk to you?"

"Just turn on the screen."

"I mean personally."

She had quarreled with Jake, and I was to be the backup again.

"Joe?"

"You mean tonight?"

"I'd like to explain."

"I really can't. . . ."

She broke the connection. I thought of calling her back, but decided against it. She was using me for something, it seemed, yet I felt she liked me also.

I went to the bathroom and washed my face with cold water. I stood there looking at my face in the mirror, wondering how I could figure Linda out if I couldn't understand myself very well.

The phone was ringing when I got back to the room.

I sat down and waited for it to stop, but it kept ringing. Finally I opened the line.

"Oh, hi," I said, surprised by Rosalie's smiling face.

"Maybe we could get together this weekend?" she asked.

I nodded.

"Are you going home for the break?"

"I don't know," I managed to say. "My folks are having problems, and they're moving."

"You're welcome at my house."

"That's very nice of you, but I can't promise."

"What's wrong?"

"Nothing much."

"Where's your roommate?"

I shrugged. "Working on his future somewhere."

"And you're not?"

I smiled. "How'd you guess?"

She was looking at me critically, but with concern. "See you this weekend." Her face faded away.

10 PROBLEMS

I did my work in a kind of trance that week. The good thing about this was I didn't notice the difficulty of the material, learning as a matter of habit, caring less each day, taking no pleasure in it. Morey was having fun, even when the work was very hard. I envied him.

Morey studied away from the room, so I saw him only when he was asleep or going somewhere. He didn't want to argue with me anymore, it seemed; his studies were more important. He was right—I did my work out of pride, because I refused to give up.

I passed Kik ten Eyck in the student center one afternoon. He gave me a puzzled look and kept walking. I saw Jake and Linda from a distance a few days after she called. Kik, of course, probably thought I wasn't good enough for his sister, since I was from Earth, but I didn't take it personally; he would have thought the same of anyone from Earth. We were all childish, overprotected types. Kik, being a tough, mature Sunspacer, preferred

Jake, who was more like himself, the brother Linda loved. It probably disturbed Kik that Linda had showed signs of being attracted to me. Still, it seemed I was missing something somewhere.

I spent a lot of time on the hillside, gazing up at the rooftops on the other side of the world. The fresh air, the soft sunlight on my face, the flowers in the grass, the impossible river rising from the lake, made my doubts seem a bad dream. . . .

Something crouched in the grass near me. A Scottish terrier's beady eyes were staring at me intently.

"Electromagnetic!" the animal squeaked, repeating some physics learned from its owner. "Explain . . . vectors, hah, hah, hah!" It laughed mockingly.

"Go on!" I shouted.

"Good-bye!" the dog cried and rushed off into the tall grass, leaving me a bit disturbed.

I lay back and wondered about the terms ahead, escaping into a future where I would be full of learning and under my own command. I pushed forward through time, watching the Earth-Moon system racing around the Sun, speeding the cosmic clock ahead into distant ages, my back pressed against the grass in this light-filled hollow. . . .

You can have anything you want in your mind, but the trick is to make dreams happen outside your head, so they become as real as the habitat around me. Still, wishes have to start deep inside you to be any good.

Rosalie found me out there, late one afternoon, when I should have been in class. She sat down next to me and took my hand.

"I don't want the distraction of getting interested in someone, not while I'm in school."

I sat up. "So why did you come out here?"

"I was worried about you. You haven't been to classes much, and that began to distract me also."

"It's okay, I'll have the grades."

She gave me an exasperated look, and I knew what she wanted to say. *Typical Earth boy. No ambition.* Kik was the kind of guy for her, I thought.

"I just don't feel the dedication for physics when it comes to work. The idea appeals to me in my head, but I don't feel it."

"Maybe you're just lazy."

I laughed. "If only that's all it was. Look—it's the wrong thing. Might as well admit it early."

"Maybe you need some time to think, Joe."

"Who knows? I'm not that unhappy about it." But when I looked at her I realized that there wasn't much in me for her to like. I hadn't done anything, and it seemed unlikely that I would.

Rosalie and I started going out on Fridays, rationing our time together so it wouldn't interfere with school. She seemed a much warmer and more sensitive person than Linda, but probably just as strong. She was determined to get what she wanted—an education before a career, in contrast to those students who thought of the university as the bottom rung of a scientific career.

I wasn't sure what Rosalie expected from me. She had a way of searching my face with her eyes for clues about my feelings. I was a little afraid she would discover a person neither of us would like.

The term ended on October 10. Morey and I got A's in our courses. He was very smug about it. Not bad for a couple of earthies.

"Good going, Joe," he said, but with a hint of doubt.

"Just a first term." Ro had pushed me a bit, but I still wasn't a true believer. Her encouragement had helped and I felt a little guilty. True believers sat around to all hours, plotting how to seize the holy grail of physics. It all depended on which problems they selected to solve; pick wrong and you were finished. So how could I do anything? I had no beastie in sight; I only got grades.

The campus became a ghost town. The Earth kids went home for two weeks; the locals stayed in their towns. I was alone in the dorm, except for some wandering maintenance people and Carlos Ramirez in 107. I tried to talk to him, but he was hard at work for the next term and didn't want to waste time. He was an orphan, studying physics on a small income from an insurance trust. He had no one on Earth except the bank. His grim determination made me feel worse about myself.

Rosalie came and stayed with me for a few days. We slept late and went swimming in the lake before noon. Ramirez always gave us a few dour looks when we came back.

"I don't think we're setting a good example," Ro said one day.

"Don't worry, he's tough. So how are your parents?" I asked as I changed my clothes.

"There's only Dad and me. He's fine."

"Oh."

She saw my hesitation. "My mother isn't dead or anything, Joe, as some people assume. Dad had me alone."

"But you have genes from two parents, don't you?" I asked, relieved that it was nothing sad.

"Sure, but the female were made up to order." She laughed. "There's no Mom hiding somewhere for me to wonder about. I know you're more used to it on Earth, but it's getting quite common out here in the habitats. After all, we pioneered the biofacilities decades ago." She smiled. "I'm healthier than chance combinations, since at least half my characteristics are handpicked. By Dad, of course."

I knew about it, but she was the first I'd met. "Were you born from a host mother?"

"No. Quality-controlled womb. What do you think?" She stepped out of her damp suit.

I put my arms around her. "You make me very happy," I said.

Ramirez pounded on the wall a few times before we went to lunch.

The Mercury talks resumed on October 17. Ro and I were hoping that there wouldn't be another quake before the negotiations were concluded. I didn't really like the idea of negotiating about such things; what was right was right. Negotiations seemed just a way for Earth to see what it could get away with doing.

I came out of the bathroom one morning and saw a familiar shape walking away from me down the hall.

"Bernie!"

He turned around and smiled. "Joe. How about seeing a bit of the engineering level?" His memory was perfect.

"Sure, when?" Ro was at the bookstore and I had nothing better to do. The break from school had put me in a good mood.

"We can go right through the dorm," Bernie piped, "and go along the water system."

He led me down the stairs into the basement, where he opened a large hatch in the utility area. I followed him down a spiral staircase. We came out into a tunnel. Guide lights went on overhead.

We got into the open track car and it whispered off

down the passage. The overhead guide light snaked ahead of us, darkening behind us.

"We're running along the water and drain pipes," Bernie said. He took a deep breath, then another.

"What's wrong?"

"Nothing. But sooner or later I'll have to have a new heart grown for me. Doc says I need a general cell scrub and 'juvenation. Getting old."

"Nobody's really old before a hundred nowadays."

"That's what they teach, but you'd be surprised how many people die in their eighties."

"Do you feel old?"

"Sometimes."

There wasn't much I could say to that. I liked him, and felt that he liked me. He'd remembered our meeting on the hill, and was eager to show me around.

"You can't see much down here in one day," he said.

"That's okay." I looked back into the dark tunnel. "Where are you from, Bernie, originally?"

"Earth. Had a son and daughter there, lost a second wife, and spent twenty years in prison. Learned enough to make myself useful when they sent me out to help build this place."

"What were you in for?" I asked, wondering if he had killed his wife.

"Computer bank theft. They never found the money."

"What did you need it for?"

"Things were worse in those days. I had a common-law wife who ran away and left me with two kids. I set the kids up for life, but the money couldn't be traced back to me. No one knew who they were or where. I had no time to raise them. I set it all up, so that when they caught me my kids would have enough. The money disappeared the day I transferred it. No one cares any-more."

"You don't mind telling me?"

"It's in my files now. I like you well enough." He looked up. "We're under the lake now."

"The sphere gets its water from the lake, I take it."

"Right. It's used to irrigate the land, since we don't get much rain weather. Land inside one of these can get very dry. The system releases water directly into the ground at thousands of points, then it drains through the ground back into the lake. Those switches have to be checked routinely and replaced when the computer says so. I can let you off at the student center on the way back, if you like."

"That's okay."

"If you're ever free, come and work for me. I'd be glad to teach you what I know."

"Are you serious about that?"

"It's the second time I've asked. Remember?"

"Don't you think I'll stay in school?"

He gave me a sly grin. "I can spot the moody ones.

Seen them come and go. Make good apprentices. It doesn't matter about school. You can work a term and go back."

"Oh." I was surprised at how sure he was about me.

"You know where to find me," he said as the car slowed to a stop near a dark exit. "Give me a minute here. All I have to do is plug in an automatic switching unit. There are spares right here on the shelf. Then I'll shoot back with you to the student center."

I wanted to see more.

"Next time," Bernie said, sensing my disappointment.

It bothered me a little to think that anyone could figure me out, especially since I was having trouble doing it myself. Were people pretty simple when they were young, growing more complicated as they grew older?

Morey came back on the twenty-third.

"You're a day early," I said almost accusingly.

"Got to get a good start. What did you do?"

"Walked around a lot. Kept to myself."

"See Rosalie Allport?"

"Once or twice," I said reluctantly.

"I'm glad to be back," he said, sounding like his old self. "Mom kept asking if I still got the whoopsies in space. She kept saying the word. They dragged me around to their friends. At home I was the kid with the whoop-sies, but in front of their pals I was the wonder brain from space. A few of their pals dislike Sunspacers. Never noticed it before. They see them as misfits who can't hack it on Earth. There's a lot of hate about the Sunspacers siding with the miners. You wouldn't have liked it. I had to come back early."

He was glad to see me. And I was happy to see him, I realized. Maybe we could get along after all.

"Did you get sick this time?" I asked, needling him.

"Funny about that, I didn't."

The second term began. We had the same teachers for the second halves of the first term's courses. I worked very hard, trying to keep to my resolve.

There was a knock on my door one afternoon in the first week.

"Come in!" I shouted.

The door slid open as I turned around, and I saw Linda. "Will your roommate be back soon?" she asked, stepping inside. The door slid shut behind her.

"I don't know."

"What are you reading?" she asked, smiling nervously.

"*War and Peace*," I said, puzzled. "Leo Tolstoy."

"I've read it. It's long."

"I know."

She looked at me uncertainly. "Joe, I want to explain why I disappeared that evening."

"You don't have to."

"I want to," she insisted.

"I understand about you and Jake."

"It's not just that. When news came that my parents had been killed in the shuttle accident, it was a call from someone who sounded like your father. I thought you were going to hear something bad. I know it's stupid, but I can't listen when I know kids and parents are going to argue. It all got mixed together that night. I'm sorry. It's been four years," she continued, "but it seems like yesterday. Kik and I have only each other."

"You must have loved them a lot," I said, standing up.

She came up to me and kissed me. "Joe," she whispered. "I wanted you that night. But that's all it was."

I stared at her. She smiled and put her arms around me, and we kissed again. Her lips softened and a flush came into her cheeks. "It's unfair," she whispered, pressing against me.

"What is?" I managed to ask.

"You're too yummy," she mumbled. We stumbled and fell on the bed. I tried to keep from laughing, not wanting to spoil her mood. No one had ever called me yummy. I felt like a dessert.

The door buzzed, but we ignored it. Then it slid open and I heard Rosalie say, "I thought I'd surprise—"

She stopped short and moved backward, triggering the door before it could close. I tried to say something,

but she turned and walked out. The door took forever
to close.

"I'm sorry," Linda said after a moment. I moved away
from her and sat on the edge of the bed.

"I'm sorry," she repeated, moving to sit next to me.

I took a deep breath. "It's okay."

She touched my arm.

"Go make up with Jake," I said resentfully.

"Don't be angry. It just happened, not because of
Jake. I kept thinking about you. . . ."

"Please go."

She kissed my cheek and stood up. All I wanted to
do was find Ro and change the hurt look on her face.

The phone rang. I waited for the door to close after
Linda, then I rushed to the desk, hoping that it was
Rosalie calling from the lounge.

I opened the line. Dad's face stared at me.

"Hello, Joe," he said after a moment.

"Oh, hi."

"What's wrong?" he asked after the delay.

I shook my head. "Just expecting another call." One,
two, three.

"I won't keep you. Just wanted to tell you that I've
got a new place here in New York and I'm back at work,
so your coming home for Christmas won't be any problem."

"What about Mom?" One, two, three.

"It's over, I'm afraid," he said heavily, "but she'll be here to clear up some business, so the three of us will be together."

"I don't know. Let me call in a day or two."

"What's to decide?"

"It's just that I have to see about a few things." I waited.

"Sounds like you don't want to come."

"Well, I didn't expect to!"

His expression caught up with my words. "What's wrong?" he asked softly, looking hurt.

"Nothing. Look, I'll call. There's plenty of time." One, two, three.

"I'll have to know, son."

"Yeah, I'll call."

He faded.

I called Rosalie. Her face appeared and disappeared. I touched in her number again.

"Ro, please!"

She stared. I had only a moment to get through to her.

"What is it?" she asked coldly.

"It's all a mistake!"

I explained nervously; it all sounded like a lie.

"I just don't know," she said finally.

"It was just a stupid accident, Ro!" I should have told her that I loved her, but suddenly I was uncertain. Here was my chance to be alone again, to think only of myself and what I would do with my life. Besides, what kind of person was she to doubt me so easily? Maybe I didn't know her at all.

"I'll have to think about it," she said, as if picking up my uncertainty. Maybe she was thinking the same thing—here was her chance to be rid of me. We hadn't had all that much time together. Did you ever try thinking in two opposite directions at once, and believing that you could do it? I was trying to live in two directions at once, studying physics but wanting something else; the thing with Linda probably looked like more of the same to Rosalie.

"I'll talk to you another time, Joe." The skeptical tone of her voice dismayed me. Maybe she was right to doubt me. She'd found me out, even though the scene with Linda meant nothing by itself.

I felt naked and alone.

I tried to catch her in Astronomies, but she always managed to leave by another exit. I tapped notes into her terminal, with no reply. It made me sick to think that I would never be able to set things right. How could this be happening?

I couldn't sleep, and began to miss more classes. It seemed that a stranger was doing the work when I studied. When I could sleep, it was an escape. Rosalie's sudden rejection of me had struck deeply. I had balanced my doubts against each other and avoided taking a good look at myself, at what I was or could be. Rosalie, I felt, was punishing me for being dishonest with myself.

"You've got to snap out of it," Morey said one Monday afternoon. He had come back from classes and found me sleeping. "You'll fail some finals and they'll kick your ass out."

"I can make up a few weeks easily."

"What's happening to you?"

I sat up on the edge of the bed. "I need time to think. Maybe I shouldn't have come here."

He tried to be encouraging. "But you can do the work. They wouldn't have let you in."

"Mistakes happen. You were right, I just don't care. It's not just Rosalie. She was right too, I'm not going anywhere. The diploma won't mean a thing, even if I get honors."

"Come on! You're not just any dodo." But he couldn't hide the contempt in his voice.

"Go away, Morey," I said, standing up and adjusting my underwear. "I don't have to listen to this crap."

He laughed at me. "You should see yourself. So tough."

I pushed him away. He staggered back.

"You think there are no other kinds of people in the world besides you," I said.

"Of course there are. Muscleheads like you."

145

"You—" I started to say, trying to keep up my steam against the sense of shame flooding into me. "You think there are heads and hands, and you're a head. The rest of us are just unfortunates."

He looked a bit embarrassed. "Well, you could be a head, but you won't be."

"Other things take heads too."

He grimaced and left the room. I felt that he had given up on me completely, and that woke me up more than anything. I didn't have to be like him; I could try to be myself.

I went over to Goddard Hall after dinner and threw a pebble at Ro's third-floor window. She turned away when she saw me, making me feel abandoned and useless.

I tossed another pebble. Kea Tanaka opened the window. Her long black hair swung forward as she leaned out. "Go away, Joe, she won't talk to you."

"I've got to," I shouted, hoping Ro would hear me. "Help me," I half whispered.

She shook her head, and I hated her unreasonably. "Try!" I urged.

"She doesn't want to see you." She waved a plump arm at me. "Go away."

Rosalie appeared next to her and closed the window without looking at me. I turned and walked away. What had it been like for Mom and Dad, who had spent so many years together?

"Joe!"

I turned around. She was standing in front of the main entrance. I hurried over. She took my arm and led me to a nearby bench.

She looked at me carefully as we sat down.

"You still don't believe me, do you?" I asked.

"I do, now, but you gave me a scare. I know Linda, even if we're not close friends. I think she doesn't break off with Jake because losing him scares her more than loving him. Don't forget, she lost her parents. She's the same way with Kik sometimes. They'd do anything for each other, but you'd never guess it from the way they act in public—very quiet or taking jabs at each other. Jake's older, so he wants Linda to make her own decisions, to stay with him because she wants to. Unfortunately, this lack of pressure on his part sometimes gives her too much space to flap around in, and she thinks he doesn't want her. Jake's been Kik's friend for a while, so he understands her and can see things coming. Linda's afraid of losing anybody she loves too much. She goes out with others to test Jake, and to see if she loves him."

"Well, I think she liked me a little . . ."

She smiled. "But not enough."

"I guess. Who knows? . . ."

147

"Look, Joe, there are more important things. What's bothering you? Don't you like school?"

"It's hard when you have the feeling that it's all not for you."

"Are you homesick?"

"Not really. I do feel out of place sometimes. The reasons I'm here don't seem to go through me—they don't reach down deep, as they do with Morey. He's having fun, even when the work is hard. I feel jealous. The work is interesting, but I take no pleasure in it."

She was quiet for a moment. "Why don't you do what I do, Joe? Get the grades and don't worry so much what you'll amount to. Don't freeze it all up in advance. Give yourself a chance to grow."

"That's what I've been doing," I insisted. "But Morey says that won't make me a star physicist. He makes me feel like a phony."

"You don't have to be Morey, Joe."

Marisa had told me the same thing once. "You're right, but what am I going to be? Is this all there is?"

"Stop being anxious about it first."

Rosalie still seemed to think that I wasn't a complete waste of time, but I had shaken her confidence in me for a while. I had been too wrapped up in my own fears to notice that she had made no sweeping judgments about me.

"Was there a girl back home?" Rosalie asked.

I nodded. "She broke it off."

"Why?"

I hesitated. "Said I was too wrapped up in myself, as if I were something special. I guess my going away to Bernal only convinced her more."

She was smiling faintly. "What do you think about yourself now?"

"Same thing I did then," I mumbled. "That I could do something special. I know it sounds stupid."

She kissed me. "You're special to me. The rest you'll have to see about."

We kissed again. "I didn't want to hurt you," I whispered, holding her close. "I love you very much."

"Same here," she whispered back.

We sat in silence for a while, and I decided to tell her. "I almost punched Morey today—I never hit anyone even in fun before, at least not since I was a little kid. Can't believe I shoved him like that." I looked at my hands as if they had betrayed me.

"But why?" she asked, not sounding too surprised.

"He was talking to me like a parent. I don't know— maybe he's right about everything but I'm afraid to admit it. Guess I'm pretty screwed up. . . ."

White clouds drifted in the bright, starless evening of the hollow. I wasn't going to solve anything right away, but with Ro next to me my fears didn't seem quite so important.

"Come spend Christmas with me," Ro said. "You won't have to go home or stay at the dorm. We'll put you up at the house."

"Okay."

"Dad's a great cook," she said.

I felt bad about Morey. We'd never even wrestled in fun. He'd probably never talk to me again, I realized. But I also felt a bit relieved; it was all out in the open now—I didn't have to follow in his footsteps. I could try to make my own, even if I didn't know where they would lead.

Morey was packing his stuff when I got back to our room the next morning.

"There's a place for me on another floor," he said. "Kid's roommate dropped out." He looked at me for a moment, clearly suggesting that I would flunk out also, then went on with his packing.

I felt anger and hurt at the same time. I wanted to apologize, but I couldn't, and it was too late to do any good.

"It's just as well," I said, trying to sound unconcerned, "I was planning to move out next term anyway."

Morey didn't reply, and I felt miserable.

11 HOLIDAYS

I wasn't able to reach Dad, so I left him a message. He called back a week later.

"Joe, what is this? Why can't you come home for Christmas?"

"I told you. Rosalie asked me to her house."

I waited.

"You didn't mention it when I talked to you."

"I forgot. Maybe I didn't know then."

He stared at me. I watched his expression catch up with my words. "That's not like you, Joe. What's going on?"

"You probably weren't planning much anyway."

He was silent for much longer than the delay.

"Sorry," I added, knowing that I was punishing him for not letting me come home for intersession.

"If you won't come, I can't force you," he said finally. His face faded away. I felt relieved and saddened.

I went to Bernie's office on the second floor of the student center, hoping to talk about taking a job with him during the next term. The message plate on the door read that he was in Riverbend Hospital for an indefinite stay.

It was a Saturday morning, so I called Ro and we arrived at the admissions desk an hour later.

"He's in cold suspension life support," the male nurse told us.

"What happened?" I asked nervously.

"Heart—he'll have to stay until his new one is grown, and for a complete cell scrub renewal. He should be out before Christmas. Do you want to see him?"

"How can we?" I asked, puzzled and afraid.

"Are you friends or relatives?"

"Friends," Ro said. "Joe knows him better than I do, but everyone has heard of Bernie at the university. He's a legend."

"Yes, I know," the tall nurse said. "Come this way. He'll need to hear from someone. We haven't been able to contact any of his family."

We followed him down a long corridor, through a few heavy doors, and into a large monitoring room.

"Number six," the nurse said, pointing to a screen.

I took a deep breath as I saw Bernie's face. It was composed, as if he were dead.

"Say something reassuring."

"Can he hear me?" I asked.

The nurse nodded. "He'll pick it up at a deep mental level. It helps calm the body, we've learned."

I leaned close to the pickup. "Bernie," I said, choking up, "this is Joe Sorby. I want you to get well soon, so I can work for you. . . ."

"His signs are calmer," the nurse said after what seemed a long silence. "He must like you."

"I've met him only a few times," I said, "but we talked a lot."

"Come back when he's through the replacement. It'll be routine. We're a bit puzzled why he didn't come in sooner. You'll help his recovery."

"Haven't you heard from his kids on Earth?" I asked.

"Not yet."

I looked closely at Bernie's face, wondering what he might be dreaming. Had he grown tired of life and decided to die when his body failed? I couldn't believe it. He was obviously needed. Or was there something I didn't know? "Get well," I repeated, swallowing hard, afraid of my feelings. We had talked about more than I realized.

"You're drawn to him," Ro said as we walked back across the bridge from Riverbend.

I looked around. "I guess I admire what he's helped do here. He can see what his life has been for. It's all around him, and he still helps keep it going."

"You'll probably enjoy working for him. I can tell in the way you say it." She smiled at me.

"Is it a good hospital?" I asked.

"Sure. His kind of recovery is routine, although

he shouldn't have let it go so long. You won't miss school?"

"It can wait."

"It's not the best I've seen," Fred Allport said as he adjusted the three-dee holo of the Christmas Tree from New York City's Rockefeller Center. He had the whole scene reduced to fit in the corner of the living room. The people ice-skating under the branches seemed like toys.

I had given Rosalie a bracelet, and had received a shirt. Fred gave us a miniature set of the Oxford Classics. Ro had stopped me from buying him anything; he had insisted that our spending time with him would be enough.

Fred was a great cook and a nonstop talker, and he never tired of showing me his books. The visit took my mind off everything for a week. I felt that he wanted me to like him, and that he was very pleased with me, for more than Rosalie's sake.

On Christmas Day there was a fireworks display in the square of each town. We sat watching from the terrace of the house as the towns tried to outdo each other. Little universes of light blossomed in the great space, throwing shadows across the countryside, illuminating the patterns of roads, houses, and backyards overhead.

"How was the term?" Fred asked as the display came to an end with a sparkle of yellow.

"Joe got all A's," Ro said.

"Very good!"

I shrugged. "So did she." I had never been praised much for success. Fred's genuine delight upset me. I felt a bit guilty about not going back next term.

The conversation drifted around to the Mercury crisis.

"They know they have to give them what they need, eventually," Fred said, massaging his forehead. "Dragging out the final agreement like this will only give the bad feelings a longer life."

Rosalie looked at me. "You are coming to the rally with me on New Year's Day, aren't you?"

"If they haven't signed the agreement by then," I said.

Fred chuckled. "Show more interest, son. My daughter is a toughie on stuff like this." His voice vibrated with his pride in her.

"Doesn't feel like they'll settle it," Ro said.

I stood up. "We'd better hurry if we're going to make the boat ride."

"Have a nice time," Fred said with a note of loneliness in his voice.

The craft crossed the lake, gliding toward the outflowing stream. Rings of moonlight trembled on the dark water. We sat on deck and watched quietly for a long time.

The boat entered the flow of the river. It would take

all evening to circle the equator and return us to the lake by the inflow stream.

A couple passed by us.

"Have you told your parents?" Rosalie asked, holding my hand.

"Not yet."

"Has Bernie found a job for you yet?"

"He will. I hope to get work with him, at least for next term."

"It'll do you good, whatever you decide later."

A slight breeze blew across the water. I watched the lights on the shore and imagined the massive circulating pumps that helped take the water in and out of the lake. Bernie had told me about it on my regular visits to him during his recovery. The water had been manufactured out of hydrogen and oxygen; it would have been very difficult to lug that much water out here when the place was built.

Rosalie slipped over to my recliner and we kissed for a while. It seemed that she was trying to tell me much more than that she loved me. She also needed me, and I felt my caring for and loyalty to her grow into a force of tenderness that could never be defeated. Kisses are sometimes whispers that you can't quite hear.

"Merk! Merk! Merk!" the crowd chanted insistently.

Riverbend's main square was jammed with people on the afternoon of New Year's Day.

Even though the rest of the solar system had sided with Mercury, and despite the fact that no one would gain by a breakdown of metal delivery into Earthspace, there was still no agreement.

I was pretty angry when I learned that the ores weren't even half the story. No one would gain—in the long run; but an embargo on space imports to Earth—a cut-off of medical products, alloys, electronics, optical surfaces, not to mention reductions in simple power transmission—would help rearrange, if not topple, many political careers, and ruin a number of business interests on the planet. So it was to the benefit of various rival groups on Earth to drag out the agreement with Mercury and ruin their enemies. Resignations had been in the news all week.

Ro and I were at the edge of the crowd. We'd gotten up late, but it was just as well; we'd have been trapped in the crowdlock, unable to move until it broke.

Making sense of the forces playing around the Mercury problem was a job in itself—a lot of it seemed as if it couldn't possibly make sense—but I tried. Short-term interests were delaying worthy long-term developments everywhere. The Asteroids were keeping more of what they produced and building habitats for a growing population; self-sufficiency was an old story for much of Sunspace. The trouble with Mercury was that its population specialized in mining the planet, not settling it; too little time and energy was left over for improving

157

the quality of life. If conditions did not improve, the miners might demand to leave and find work on Mars and in the Asteroids; those growing communities would be happy to have them. So the only way to keep the Mercury families put was to give them a habitat.

Mercury's resources would last for centuries, Bernie had pointed out when we had visited him during his recovery; so it made sense to develop the place. A habitat would stimulate free trade. Mercury's space would become a more humane place to live and work.

Earthside politicos had always hated the planet's increasing dependence on the civilization beyond the sky. But it wasn't Earth's fault that it lacked the conditions for a humane industrialism. Its renunciation of destructive industries had saved the planet's environment, and was a natural development for humankind—a move from a finite industrial base to a practically unlimited one.

"But the principal product of Earth is still people," Bernie had insisted during our long talks in the hospital. "It can nurture, educate, and supply them wherever they may be needed. Someday Sunspace will all be one, and Earth will be the name given to all the inhabited space around the Sun."

Bernie had looked very good by the end of his hospital stay. He stood up straighter when they let him out of bed; his skin looked younger, his hair thicker. His eyes seemed more penetrating and critical; his speech was quicker. It was heartening to see. I was happy for him, and it pleased Rosalie to see us become good friends.

The crowd quieted as the holo projector cast a giant figure in front of the courthouse. The man gazed down at the crowd, as if preparing to stomp us with his feet.

The crowd booed. "That's LeCarrier," Ro shouted to me, "the chief negotiator!"

The titanic ghost raised its arms. "We have a settlement!" his voice boomed.

"About time!" a smaller voice replied.

"Booooo!"

LeCarrier looked exasperated. "We have a settlement," he repeated as the crowd calmed down. "And some other good news. An asteroid hollow has been diverted from its Martian orbit into a powered sunward trajectory. It should be in Mercury's space within a few months."

The gathering gave a feeble cheer.

"We are taking applications for volunteers who will be needed during the construction of the asteroid interior. No conscript or convict labor will be used, not even youthful offenders."

The crowd cheered more loudly. A sense of relief and satisfaction rushed through me. Rosalie put her arm around my waist. "Finally, it's over," she said.

"We've won!" someone shouted, sending a jolt through me and the crowd. "Merk! Merk! Merk!" the massed voices chanted, breaking up into whistles, cheers, and hoots. "We've won!"

LeCarrier looked even more exasperated, but he smiled. I had the feeling that he did not like the outcome; it had made clear, perhaps too strongly, that power was shifting from Earth to its offspring.

The figure of LeCarrier winked out and was replaced by another—a middle-sized man with black hair, combed straight back, sitting in a bare room. He didn't seem old, only tired.

"Robert Svoboda," Ro whispered, "the head man on Mercury."

Again I felt a thrill, knowing that I was looking at someone very special.

"I'd like to thank the additional negotiators on Earth," he said softly, then paused and looked around, as if listening for something. For a moment it seemed that he was examining the hollow of Bernal. His image trembled. "A minor quake," he said finally. It seemed that he wanted to say more, but he only smiled, waved, and faded away.

"I hope nothing more happens before the agreement is fulfilled," Ro said, holding me close. "A lot can happen before then."

I looked at her carefully and realized what she was thinking. "You want to go, don't you?" I asked.

She nodded. "Don't you? You will come if I go, won't you?" She sounded unsure.

I hesitated, even though I knew I would want to go. "Sure, if they take us." My voice trembled a bit. It would be a big step, and dangerous, unlike anything I'd ever known to sail against the solar wind to the first planet, which whipped around the blinding center of all Sunspace.

"They'll take us," Ro said finally.

"I got this notice from the University," Dad said, "that you're taking the term off."

"I need some time." One, two, three.

"You've only been two terms! What's wrong?"

"Nothing. I need time to think."

"But tell me why," he said after the pause.

I felt my pulse race. What could I tell him? That maybe I didn't want to go back ever? "I'll probably go back next term."

Dad sighed after a moment. "Your mother will blame me."

"You had nothing to do with it."

"She blames me for everything I can't control."

"You're wrong," I said. "She blames you for *trying* to control everything, to keep things steady and calm, to suit yourself. You still don't understand, do you? This is my decision to make. Mom probably felt the same way when she decided to break away. You've got to understand that."

"What will you do?" he asked finally, and it seemed that my point had sunk in.

"I think I have a job for the term."

"Doing what?"

"Maintenance apprentice."

"Apprentice? Doesn't that require a longer commitment?"

"If I want it."

He was shaking his head, making me very nervous. "Joe, Joe, this is not for you."

"Why not?" I demanded.

He stared. My words caught up with him and he still stared. "What are you saying? You just said for the term."

"Probably." I should have kept my mouth shut. "I'll just have to wait and see."

He was silent.

"Dad, it'll be okay," I insisted, "believe me."

Mom called a few minutes later.

"Joe, are you really going to do this?"

"I'll be fine, don't worry." There was no way they could stop me.

She took a deep breath. "When did you think of this?"

"I need the time off, Mom." One, two, three.

"You'll just lose time."

"It's not wasting time to consider what I want."

My words seemed to crawl across space.

"You could do that while finishing school."

"Come on, Mom, saying it won't make it work."

She glared at me. "I'll call back after your father and I discuss what to do."

I got angry. "You can't scare me, Mom. I didn't say anything when you two separated. That was your own business. Why can't you leave me alone?" I felt terrible saying it, as if I were a criminal.

They'll get used to the idea, I thought as she faded away.

The phone rang again.

"Joe—why don't you just come home?" Dad said as he faded in. "You won't have to work. You'll rest up and we can talk, and we . . . you could visit your mother." And report back to you, I said to myself silently. "Well?"

"But I want to work, Dad." One, two, three.

"You don't have to."

"And I want to stay here."

"Is it someone—a girl?" he asked after the pause.

"That's only part of it."

He stared. "Oh—Eva thought you didn't want to come home because we weren't together."

"It wouldn't make any difference."

He seemed relieved. "Did you get the money we put in your account for Christmas?"

"Sure did. Thanks. By the way, I got A's."

"Great! Eva thought it might have been your studies."

"She could have asked." One, two, three.

"We're not ourselves, Joe. It's hard to start life again, alone."

"I guess."

There was a knock on my door.

"Call you next week, Dad. I've got to go." I hung up and turned around. "Come in!"

The door slid open and Bernie came in. He sat down on my bed and wiped his forehead with his sleeve. "I've been running all day and doing zero. You've got the job, by the way."

"What's the matter?" I asked, sitting back in my chair.

"Building Trades Guild complains I haven't been training enough apprentices."

"You've been sick!"

"I could work full time again. Passed my new physical, so they can't do a thing."

"Then what's wrong?"

He looked at me with lips pressed together. "Their trying to retire me hurts," he piped, "even if the attempt failed. Can't slow down or be sick without someone fishing for your job."

"Don't you work directly for Bernal?"

164

"I work for the Town Councils. They trust my word, even though Artificial Intelligence Brain's monitors say the same. But the Guild claims any inspector can do as well, that *all* I do is agree with the sensors. Who do they think installed those mites in the first place, or replaced most of them at least once? I know every link and cable, and I have a way of talking to the AI Brain so it tells me things without knowing."

It was never work for Bernie, I realized. He was afraid that one day something stupid would be decided and he would lose a way of life; for him it would be the same as dying.

He gestured over his shoulder with his thumb and seemed to breathe easier. "I look out from my house mornings and feel good that the whole inside is green and living, that the towns have electric and water. We built this world out here in the middle of nothing at all. It catches the Sun, gives people a place to live and poke at the universe from."

There was a renewed hope and joy in what he said, pointing to a whole universe outside my problems. It was obvious that he was completely recovered.

"Will I be working for you, Bernie?"

"If nothing goes wrong." He gazed at me with his youthful blue eyes, then scratched his white curls. "Go down to the town hall and register as soon as you can. Are you over sixteen?"

"I'm seventeen."

He put out his hand. I reached over and shook it. "You're not an apprentice, though, not unless you sign a contract."

"I know."

"It'll be nice to work with you, Joe."

I smiled. "Same here, Bernie."

I felt bad not telling him it would only be till Ro and I left for Mercury.

12 WORKING

All during January I watched Bernie work, helping him as I learned. We crawled into every nook and cranny of the colony—under the housing complexes, under the open land, checking the ecosystems, electrical conduits, neutrino-sensor links, water and ventilation passages. It brought home to me how necessary the service level was to Bernal's survival and well-being. The same was true of any building ever built, so there was nothing special about Bernal except the details.

But what details! There was an average of five feet of soil, more than enough for rose gardens and trees; then twenty feet of service level, followed by fifty of outer shell, mostly tons of slag shielding and water-filled cavities as a guard against meteor penetration and hard solar radiation. The slag was left over from Lunar mining processes, hurled into L-5 space by the Moon's mass thrower—a big bucket on a fast track. There would always be enough materials, for as many habitats and manufacturing centers as the Sunspacers cared to build.

Bernie not only liked to check when something was wrong—when the Brain picked up a sensor alarm—but he also liked to just nose around. He carried thousands of possible trouble spots in his head, and some part of him was always thinking about what might go wrong.

Of course, he wasn't the only one who knew a lot about the place, but many of the others were no longer on Bernal. Bernie didn't want to live anywhere else; the whole place was alive in his mind.

"You don't have to, Joe," he said to me one day. We were on our knees, staring down into one of the water cavities. A sensor had died, denying us readings of heat changes in the outer shell, as the big ball turned in and out of direct sunlight. Bernal's rotation averaged out the temperature in the outer shell, but the heat exchanges weren't perfect.

"The water may be frozen near the bottom," Bernie said. "One damaged sensor isn't crucial, but it can probably be repaired rather than replaced."

"I'll get it."

He gave a tug on the sensor's line. "It's stuck about twenty feet down."

I put on the mask, adjusted the rebreather pack on my back, and jumped in.

The water was cool, but it got colder as I pulled myself lower. The light beam from my mask played on the cable. The water was gray-blue, foggy.

I pulled lower, shivering as I imagined that I would reach Bernal's outer shell and look out into space, where Earth and Moon swam in a black sea. It was strange to realize that I was swimming toward the stars.

A milky surface lay below me. I reached the floor of ice and saw where the floating sensor had been caught by the freeze. Taking out a small pick, I chipped away until the small device came loose. Bernie whisked the unit away when I tugged on the line.

I cast my beam in a circle, looking to see what else might need tending, then pushed off from the bottom. I was beginning to get cold by the time I surfaced.

"Not much to fix," Bernie said. "Just a plug-in and we can drop it back on a shorter line." He was rummaging around in his tool bag for the replacement part as I climbed out. "Good going, Joe. Anything else?"

"No," I said as my teeth began to chatter. But it felt good to do something and see the use of it right away— no waiting for distant moments of achievement that might never come, as Morey would have to do. I still felt a bit guilty about Morey. You have no faith in yourself, he would probably say. But working with Bernie made me feel good about myself, and I needed that.

Several times a month Bernie sat before his terminal and punched what he knew—observations, drawings, suspicions—into Bernal's Brain. He loved the colony and was trying to put his whole mind into the central banks of the cyber-intelligence. He was part of the settlement, as much as the recyclers and solar power plants.

The administrators had long ago learned to let Bernie do all the checking he wanted. He often seemed a pest to the younger bureaucrats, but was too frequently right to be ignored. Bernie was a natural resource, a maker of traditions; and if the cyber-intelligences ever became the equals or superiors of the human mind in creative capacity, it would be because they had been weaned and raised by people like Bernie.

I rented a room in Bernie's house. There were fifty such modular houses in the North Low-G Park, mostly single-floor blocks in an open, grassy area with scattered trees. Bernie owned his house, but many of the other tenants were skilled transients, working at specialized short-term jobs in the space factories near Bernal. Some were planning to go on to the Moon, Mars, the Asteroids—wherever they got the best offers. Most were from Earth, having come out under one kind of contract or other. There were married couples, brothers and sisters, teams of siblings and parents, as well as bands of men and women brought together only by skills—all hoping to make it in off-planet industries. Very few would climb high in the companies and agencies for which they worked, but the pay and benefits were good, the opportunities for education excellent. The work was often dangerous, but there was more of it than could ever be done by the number of applicants.

I thought little about going back to school. I had a lot of respect and affection for Bernie, and he said I was good at what I did. The tiredness at the end of each workday freed me from the pressure of worrying about the future. I felt like someone else; my name was just a tag from the past, like my shirt or shoe color. What is it that makes you what you are? Maybe we have to be forced to learn what we're good at, and that marks us for life, not what we *think* we are or should be.

I had little time for reading, except as part of the job. I would go over to Cole Hall and have dinner with Rosalie. Between seeing her and the job, I had no time for anything, not even for worrying if I had been crazy to sign up for Merk. It sometimes occurred to me that I was happy here. So why was I going? Because I still thought I was special and could make a difference. Old ideas die hard.

Bernie came home one Saturday afternoon in March and sat down in the old chair facing the sofa, where I was taking a nap. I usually lounged around on my day off, watching newscasts from Earth, waiting for Ro to give me a call when she was done with schoolwork.

Bernie stared at me strangely, and I wondered if what

he had to say would make it harder for me to tell him my news.

I sat up. "What is it? You look as if you'd been chased by the Brain's ghost on the engineering level."

He smiled feebly. "It's not that. They're sending me to Merk, to work on the habitat."

"Oh." For a moment I had thought it was something really bad. "Don't you want to go?"

"I should. They need people who can do things well."

"Then what's wrong?"

He shook his head. "It's bad out there. The way it's been is Earth gets various ores while getting rid of un-desirables. But there are children and young people out there now who will have it even harder if the habitat isn't built well."

I could see he was being pulled two ways. He liked being needed for a worthy project, but he didn't want to leave home. Maybe the hospital stay had taken something out of him. For the first time since I had met him, I felt a moment of disappointment.

"I should go," he repeated, "even if the working conditions aren't perfect." He looked at me and I felt that I had missed the point. But then it all dawned on me, and I knew that I would surprise him.

He took a deep breath. "I was hoping . . . that you'd apprentice with me and we'd go together. I would need you."

We stared at each other.

"A lot of kids your age are going," he said before I could tell him. He looked down at the carpet.

"Bernie—Ro and I have volunteered."

He looked up and smiled, and I saw how much he had become attached to me. "But don't you plan to go back to school?" He had thought that I would refuse.

I shrugged. "Not just yet."

"But will you apprentice with me? No one wants to sign if it means going to Mercury."

"What else is going on? Tell me."

"Well, the agreement calls for a certain number of workers to be sent, and there just aren't that many volunteers who qualify, not yet anyway. They just about said I would have to go, if only to be able to come back and keep my position here."

"They threatened you?"

He nodded. "Why should I protest? It's a good cause. Bernal can get along without me now."

"Bernie!"

"I know, I know. Earth Authority has people here, pressuring the Guilds. I get an apprentice and go, or I don't work again."

"It's wrong," I said, appalled. "How can they?"

"They'll force my retirement—even if they have to invent a charge. It would be a lot of trouble for me to fight, even if it didn't stick. There's a lot of push to get this job done, Joe. The pressure's on from the top down to raise the skilled work force. Earth has to have the resources and it's gotten tired of the guilt publicity."

"And you still want to go?" I was ready to go punch someone.

"What Earth Authority thinks doesn't matter. I should go, and I should take an apprentice with me. There aren't enough people. The work will be useful and challenging."

"You'll have me with you," I said, feeling angry that this wonderful man was being pushed around to do what he would have agreed to anyway.

Ro and I were finishing dinner on the terrace of Cole Hall. The dinner hour was over, so we were alone.

"I knew he would probably go," she said after I had told her about Bernie. "They'll need thousands of people before it's over, and they don't have enough to even start. The pay they're offering doesn't compare with other things, so they're using pressure to get people, wherever they can."

"It's going to be a big step for the two of us. I wonder what we're getting into."

"I'm hoping we won't have to leave before the term ends," Ro said. "I don't like incompletes."

She stared at me from across the small table, and I

174

wondered if I was going because of her, or Bernie, or to get away from school. Or maybe I just wanted to see far places and do something worth doing; maybe this was what I'd been waiting for all along, without knowing it. Maybe Earth Authority was right—the job had to be done, and the fact that it would inconvenience individuals just wasn't as important; that's what happens when you wait too long in solving problems.

"I'm glad we're going together," Ro said, touching my hand. "I was sure you'd go. You wouldn't have been the person I know if you had refused. I know we can't be one-hundred-percent sure about doing this—no one could be. But I know it's right and we're doing the best we know can be done. What else can anyone do?"

She was right. I pushed my doubts aside. The project sang to me; it would be both exciting and useful.

I was sure enough.

"But why should *you* go?" Dad asked.

The question made me angry. "Maybe some of us should accept responsibility for conditions created by those who came before us—especially when we *can* change things." One, two, three.

"What?"

I thought he was going to laugh.

"Joe—you and I had *nothing* to do with this!"

I felt foolish, but I tried to answer him. "Don't you see? Mercury has been one of the prices of having a Sunspace civilization. It didn't have to be that way, but that's what happened. We'll have a worse future to be responsible for if we don't act." I waited.

He grew pale. "That's a lot of propaganda. It'll get done without you, Joe. You don't have to be a hero."

"I want to go," I said sternly.

"Do you really?" he said after the delay.

"Look around you," I shouted, "at all the metal products. The alloy in your tieclip probably started in a furnace on Mercury."

"Oh, I see," he replied, ignoring my point, "maybe your friends are going. Girlfriend?"

"I have to go, Dad," I insisted, clenching my teeth.

"Think for yourself. You don't have to do what they do."

"I'm signing tomorrow. Look, Dad, I wasn't sure about going back to school just yet anyway. It's a good cause and I'll learn a lot."

A reasonable tone didn't work on him either. My words caught up with him, souring his expression further.

"It's my decision anyway," I added, "even if it's wrong." One, two, three.

"Eva will blame me," he said sadly. "Don't expect me to call and tell her."

"Are you worried about me or yourself?" One, two, three.

"That's not fair, Joe."

"There was no answer when I called her."

He was very nervous now. "It may take longer than they say."

"Take it easy, Dad, I'll be fine."

"They're just delivering bodies," he muttered, "just to fulfill the agreement."

"But it still has to be done," I insisted. "People are dying out there, and I want to do something about it!"

"What can you do?" he asked after the pause.

"I've learned a few things working." One, two, three.

He gave me a hurt, hopeless look. "You don't need my permission," he said finally, "so why talk to me about it?"

I took a deep breath. "Okay—but you can wish me luck. I'm going for personal reasons and because I want to, because it has to be done. I can't imagine not going. Can you understand that? There are just too many good reasons. I wouldn't be the person I thought I was—a person who can make a difference—if I stayed."

He sighed heavily and nodded. "Get ahold of your mother. And keep in touch."

There was a defeated look in his eyes as he faded away.

At the Riverbend Courthouse I learned that I had to contract for a year plus travel time and unforeseen delays. I would not be able to quit.

A bored-looking judge took my handprint. The contract was with Earth Authority, which now governed all employment connected with the Mercury agreement. My contract carried a fine of a hundred thousand New Energy Dollars. Acceptable reasons for breaking it were all listed, the judge said, and there were no others. They came down to two things—illness or death.

"Could you pay the fine?" she asked coldly.

"No."

"Since you cite work experience with Mr. Kristol, I'm assigning you to him. You must accept."

"That's fine with me."

She gave me a stern look. "Name of anyone who could take your place in case of legitimate cancellation?"

I shook my head. "Don't know anyone who'd want to."

She thumbed her console. My ID card jumped out at me. "Memorize the numbers."

As I left the chamber, I imagined the judge checking off another name on her quota list. Five thousand workers. Get them any way that's legal. Press gangs in the year 2057, or the nearest thing, Dad would have said, exaggerating. But it didn't matter, I told myself. It couldn't.

Rosalie met me outside. "You look glum," she said,

taking my arm as we walked toward the bridge. Our four shadows seemed crowded on the pavement. "Think of what we'll see, things we might never get a chance to know otherwise. A year isn't anything."

I felt a bit trapped, but I smiled. "Let's go make love in zero-g."

13 ACROSS THE DARK

The Mercury transports weren't ready to go until the spring term ended, which gave Rosalie a chance to finish but meant more delay for the miners; fortunately, there had been no life-threatening quakes during the wait.

A group of us, mostly student volunteers, gathered at the North Polar Dock on the first Sunday in April. Bernie wanted me to travel with the students, even though officially I was with him and entitled to share more private quarters. We took only small toilet kits; everything else would be provided on the job, they said.

I hung in the zero-g waiting area, looking around to see if I knew anyone, wondering why Mom had never replied to the letter I had left in her message memory when I had not been able to reach her. Maybe she wasn't checking her mail, or assumed I knew what I wanted and didn't need advice. Her silence bothered me. I felt a bit lost and lonely. It was strange leaving Bernal, after having wanted to come here so much in the first place.

I turned and Rosalie was at my side. She seemed strange and dreamy, maybe a bit unsure of herself.

"It's too late now," I said as we moved to board the shuttle that would take us out to the big ship. She was silent as we floated in through the hatch and found handholds in the main bay. This was just a big empty area some twenty feet across, where passengers or cargo were put for short hops from dock to ship or between habitats. L-5 factory workers used these to commute from the residential habitats, of which Bernal was the largest.

There was a porthole near my handgrip. I felt a gentle push and watched Bernal move away. It covered the whole view, but then the shuttle turned and I saw the Mercury ship—five hundred feet of silver teardrop shining in the starry black, growing larger as we crept closer.

The *H. G. Wells*, Number 97 of Earth Authority's Sunspace Fleet, was bigger than most interplanetary transports. Its pulsed fission-to-fusion nuclear engine was an older design, but still capable of pushing the vessel to velocities of well over 150,000 meters per second. That meant that the solar system from Mercury to Jupiter could be crossed in a hundred days. Mercury, Venus, Mars, never took longer than thirty days, depending on where they were in their orbits relative to

Earth. Since Merk was still going to be this side of the sun during our travel time, our trip would take about ten days. Paths taken by this kind of ship were nearly straight lines that cut across the gravitational fields of the planets; its capacity for continuous boost put the ship outside the slowing effects of the solar system's usual dynamics.

The teardrop covered the whole sky as we drifted into the forward lock. Air hissed as the hatches opened. Ro and I and the others pulled out, passing into the large vessel.

The *Wells* had twenty-five decks, each facing forward, so that during acceleration there would be from a half to one g for passengers; not real gravity, but a steady boost pushing us down on the decks.

We pulled aft through the core passage.

"University volunteers, deck four," a woman's voice instructed over the com.

I tugged on the rail and coasted into a brightly lit area. The deck itself was ahead of us, looking like a bulkhead wall with a hundred acceleration couches attached to it. Everyone was talking loudly as they hung on the handrails, which shot across the open space. Some of the faces looked familiar, but there was no one I knew. Most of the blue-green coveralls and boots were stiffly new, I noticed, unlike my own work uniform.

Someone jostled me from behind. "Excuse me," I said,

reaching for a bit of the rail. Rosalie was looking a bit uncomfortable for some reason.

"Joe!"

I turned and saw Linda. She was looking at me as if she had never seen me before.

"What is it?" I asked loudly.

She glanced at Ro before answering. "What happened to you? You haven't been in school."

"I needed some time off," I said.

Kik and Jake floated over, looking friendly. I was almost glad to see them.

"So we're all going," Jake said, sounding as if he approved.

Linda was watching me carefully. Kik was smiling.

"Let's settle in," Ro said.

We all pulled over to the deck-wall.

"These two, Joe," Ro said, pointing to the end of the fourth row. I floated over until my back was to the couch and strapped in. Rosalie took the end seat and we brought them up to a sitting position, but it still seemed that I was sitting with my ass on the wall. The feeling started to disappear as the crowd strapped in and I began to see the surface behind me as a deck; after all, who was I to argue with a hundred people who were clearly sitting on it. When everything is upside down, it all looks normal, unless you're the exception.

"Mind if I sit here?" Jake asked, taking the couch at my left.

"Go ahead," I said, glancing down the row toward Linda. She and Kik had taken the other end seats.

"She wants to sit with her brother for a while," Jake explained. "We'll switch later."

"Fine with me." I glanced at Ro. She didn't seem to care.

"Thanks." Jake seemed a bit somber.

The com crackled. "Fasten up—we'll be boosting in five minutes." The woman's voice sounded deeper.

Rosalie and I joined hands. Jake cleared his throat and shifted in his straps. I thought about the letters I had sent Morey. My going to Mercury would baffle him. I took a deep breath. We were all becoming different people.

I wished that he had answered the letters I had left in his terminal.

"Why didn't they just build better living quarters on Mercury itself?" a girl's voice asked behind me.

"They couldn't be sure," a male voice answered, "not with the way the planet was being torn up. Still is."

"What do you mean?"

"They might have to mine where they build."

The quakes, I thought, mention the damned quakes.

"Well, you know, people want what other people have. They see holos of Bernal and it looks like paradise."

184

"If you feel like that, then why are you going?" she asked.

Jake grimaced as I looked over at him.

"The Sun's real big from Merk."

"Keep your hands to yourself. You're making fun of me."

I tuned them out. A deep rumble grew in my guts.

"Here we go," Jake said.

Acceleration began to press me into the couch. The forward bulkhead started to look like a ceiling. The rumble reached a set pitch and stayed there.

I looked at Ro. She smiled. We were on our way to make a world, almost from scratch, for those who didn't have one. It was my dream come true, but from another direction. Sure, there would be plenty of big engineers to run the show, but that wouldn't make it easy. I had learned enough working with Bernie to have some idea of what it would take, and that it would take longer than expected. I had seen too much of what went wrong on Bernal, day to day, to believe that world building and maintenance was all routine.

"You will be able to move around the ship as soon as we reach one g," the woman's voice announced.

The ship was moving across the dark toward the Sun— the open-hearth fusion furnace at the center of our solar system, source of radiant and gravitational energy for the planets, dozens of moons, and countless asteroids.

I saw Sunspace as a vast gravitational maelstrom of matter and light energy. . . .

"That was probably the captain," Ro said.

"What do you suppose she's like?" I asked.

"Arrogant, proud," Jake answered. "They're above everything, and they love their ships. It's necessary that they think that way, to keep on top of their jobs. You would too if you ran billions of horses of raw energy across the sky."

"But they're not exactly unique," I said. "There's also the national space navies."

"Earth Authority's Fleet people hate the military. Toy ships are not economically productive. Of course, the military does test a lot of new technology, but—"

"I wish there were a screen in here," Ro said.

"What do you want from a refitted cargo ship?" Jake asked. "Notice the smell in here?"

Jake no longer seemed as strange to me as when I had first met him.

"What is it?"

"Probably goats," he replied, "some cows. They shipped breeding stocks in here, for Mars most likely."

A green light blinked on over the hatch in what was now the ceiling, according to my feet, signaling that acceleration was now stable. A spiral stair wound down from the deck above.

"Decks one to six for passengers," the captain said. "Please don't attempt to visit any others."

I looked over and saw Linda talking intently to her brother.

The lounge and recreation deck, two down, was another large drum-shaped chamber, mostly empty except for storage closets around the edge. A few of the kids were already taking out games, readers, and folding tables when Ro and I arrived.

"There's a screen," Ro said, pointing to the large oval plate bolted to the floor between two closets; a long cable snaked out from under it and disappeared into a utility conduit in the wall. We went over and turned it on.

The L-5 sector was a black nest filled with diamonds, emeralds, and rubies. I could see over a hundred objects—factories, research spheres, construction shacks, ship-frame docks, and solar generating plants.

I felt dizzy. The press of steady acceleration gave a sense of weight that seemed different from Bernal's spin force—no coriolis, for one thing—and I imagined that my inner ear had somehow noticed and was adjusting.

Rosalie pulled over two airbags and we sat down. As the deck filled up with people, I gazed at the screen, wondering when we would return to L-5.

"You okay?" Ro asked.

"It's passing."

I felt a bit cynical as I looked around. Sure, many of the people on board probably cared about what they were going to do, but others were going for the money, to help their work records, or to get away from various personal problems, or because recruiters had talked them into it. I wondered how certain I could be of my own motives.

Yellow-white sunlight flooded the room with an electric glare, giving us all black shadows.

"Turn down that screen!" someone shouted.

Jake approached the screen and cast a winged creature with his hands, making the shadow flap around, but I was suddenly in no mood to enjoy it. This was a bigger step than coming to Bernal. Some of my old doubts seemed to be stirring, and again I felt like a stranger to myself.

Pieces of my face broke free and floated away. I tried desperately to catch them, but there were too many. . . .

The dream pressed in tightly. I heard a whisper.

"Joe!" It was Rosalie.

I opened my eyes and sat up, listening to the ship's distant growl.

"Go back to sleep," I said.

"Shut up, Sorby," a male voice said behind me.

I lay back and dozed, feeling shut in. I would be locked up with these people for two weeks, and then I would have to work with them on Mercury for at least a year—in the space around Mercury, to be accurate.

I turned my head and saw Rosalie looking at me, and

it seemed wondrous that she could know how I felt about anything. I touched her cheek, realizing that I loved her without a doubt, and that I would have come with her even if there had been no other good reason.

I was falling, my stomach told me suddenly.

Then I bumped my head.

People were laughing and talking loudly.

I opened my eyes. The ceiling was only a few inches in front of me. I pushed away and turned to see the whole chamber filled with floaters. Rosalie drifted below me.

I grasped a rail and pulled myself to her.

"They shut the drive down for minor repair," she said.

"Who undid my strap?"

"You were floating when I woke up."

I looked around, trying to catch the prankster's eye.

"Strap in," the captain ordered. "Boost will resume in three minutes."

Ro and I pulled ourselves into our couches and fastened up. I yawned. She smiled at me. We waited.

I felt the soft vibration in my stomach. It seemed slightly different, less of a growl, smoother. Weight crept into my body.

When the green light went on, I unstrapped and stood up, hoping to make the toilet before the line got too long.

"Feel better today?" Ro asked, stretching appealingly.

"I'll be okay."

The toilets were just off the main chamber. I walked over and stood on line behind some ten people.

"How's it going, pal?" Jake asked from behind me.

"Fine," I said.

Jake looked sulky.

"What is it?" I asked.

He shook his head. "This ship is not in the best shape. Even the captain sounds nervous."

"Do you think it's dangerous?"

"Who knows?" he said softly. "Junk heaps have been known to hold together. We'll only know if it doesn't."

My turn came. I went inside and brushed my teeth, then stripped and took a shower while my clothes were cleaned.

"Hey, kid!" Jake called from the next stall. "Imagine we lose our g force now. Hah, hah!"

"Hurry up in there!" someone shouted.

Breakfast was served three decks down. The floor was white. We sat ten-a-table. A large wall screen showed the stars, Earth/Moon, and a small sliver of the Sun. I had eggs, oatmeal, juice, and coffee. Rosalie sat across from me, but we didn't feel much like talking. Not enough privacy.

I thought of Dad as I ate. Old problems, drawing

farther away. New problems drive out old ones, whether you've solved them or not; that was the only way it was ever going to be. . . .

I noticed Linda and Kik. They were not aware of anyone as they talked.

Rosalie and I began to feel more at ease in the group. We didn't care who was listening after a few days. We were all on the ship together, and that was all there was to it. People grow less impressed with each other through familiarity, even if you're very special. Some people will say anything in front of you after a while.

"You'd be good-looking if your ears weren't so big," I heard a girl say, and she was not joking; it was true, I saw, when I looked at the boy.

Dinner on the third day was some kind of beefy stuff with leafy greens in a gooey sauce. It was a shock after the better meals. The cook apologized, promising that if we ate this batch it would not happen again; it sounded like blackmail.

The air smelled of the stuff that night, making it hard to sleep. Most of us woke up looking glum, wondering if this shabbiness was a sign of worse things to come.

We got used to the routine: three meals, sitting around in the rec area staring out into space; exercising in the gym; reading, watching broadcasts from Earth. A few couples managed to steal some privacy in the showers from time to time.

Earth was very proud of itself. From the broadcasts, you could almost feel like thanking it for creating such a bad situation on Merk, just so Earth Authority could do something noble about it.

"What a load of slag!"

I turned and saw a short, stocky guy with white hair and pale complexion—the kid with the big ears—sitting with Kik. Everyone in the rec room looked bored.

"Don't knock slag shielding," said a tall, thin girl with closely cropped red hair. "It keeps you from growing funny critters on your skin when the Sun smiles at you," she added with obvious perversity. I wondered if she meant that Earth had to shield itself from the pain of truth, or was simply babbling.

"Did you ever notice," the white-haired boy continued, "how people care for their health, clothes, underwear, but not for what's in their heads? Probably the dumbest species in the universe."

"We've still got you," the girl said.

There was some feeble laughter. I wondered what it would be like to see myself from outside. Would I like myself? Would I think that I would ever be anything? Maybe I was the villain in someone else's story? Who was the hero? Maybe there are no heroes or villains, and we're all stuck somewhere between beast and angel.

Things could be dumber and harder than I thought—too hard for the kind of human being I knew. Life was simple and complicated at different times, even at the same time.

What are you anyway? You look into your eyes and imagine the grayness in your skull, and you feel alien. You might easily not have existed, but here you are, gazing out of soft gray matter with watery eyes, examining yourself and the stars, wondering at the darkness, which would be complete if there were no eyes. . . .

I got up, deciding to visit Bernie on the engineers' deck.

14 MERCURY

The *Wells* reached maximum speed, eating up the light minutes toward the center of the solar system. The Sun grew larger on our screens. As we crossed the orbit of Venus, the shrouded planet was a half-disk mirror catching the Sun. Human beings were on Venus also, probing from orbital stations, living in its clouds aboard high-atmospheric islands, exploring the hostile surface. Venus was a place of new dreams, constructive wishes that would one day change the planet into another Earth— if human beings could ever decide where they best liked to live, on planets or in free space habitats. I didn't think they would ever decide, and why should they? Life would always make a niche for itself, as it always had, wherever and whenever possible. Human beings would live inside the Sun if they could.

Mercury was just swinging in front of the Sun, becoming a dark spot as it crept across the solar face. Planetfall was still days away, but I felt a rising sense of expectation as Mercury grew on our screens. There were fewer fights among us, less bickering. We were looking forward to getting there and starting work.

On the day before arrival, one hundred fifty of us crowded into the rec room. Ro and I found ourselves in the middle, sitting on the deck. The chatter grew louder as we waited for the meeting to start. I looked around and saw Bernie standing with some of the engineers near the spiral stair. Something was very wrong and we were going to be told about it.

"What could it be?" Rosalie whispered.

There was a sudden lull. A small, thin woman in a white uniform was making her way to the screen. Her hair was gray, short, but her face was youthful, with high cheekbones and a small nose. Captain Maria Vinov seemed to be holding her anger in check.

She turned by the screen and her gray eyes searched the room. "I don't know quite how to tell you this," she said in a low, slightly hoarse voice, as if she'd just come from a shouting match, "but I will have to leave you off at the mining complex on Mercury's surface. The hollow asteroid has not arrived and is not expected to arrive in Mercury's space for at least three more weeks, due to delays and course corrections."

"And the construction sphere?" one of the engineers called out.

"Those quarters are with the asteroid. I've been told

that the hollow is in the fastest possible powered orbit, but I have no way to check. In any case, I can't stay here just to provide living quarters, because I have to pick up the next load of workers. The housing at the mining sites is adequate for the short time you'll be there. You'll get to see why you're here. But if anyone wants out, you can return with this ship and come back on a later one, assuming you're not breaking your contract. That ticket will come out of your pay, of course, since Earth Authority is picking up *one* round trip tab per contract. I don't need to remind you that a broken contract will mean an exorbitant fine." She was trying to discourage us, but I could see she didn't like it.

Kik stood up and said, "You clearly don't approve of leaving us on the surface."

"Yeah!" a male voice shouted. "The contract *said* living quarters off the surface."

Sure, I thought, but they didn't say *when* those quarters would be available.

"I have no choice," Vinov said. "You can file a case for contract violation against Earth Authority, but you'll probably have your quarters before it's settled. Returning with me may cost you more than the fine, even if you win." She looked around the deck, locking eyes with me for an instant, and I saw that she knew what this foul-up could mean. "Anyone coming back?"

We're stuck, I thought in the silence.

196

"One of the engineers, Mr. Denny Studdy, will give you a brief orientation." She nodded to us and made her way out, leaving us uneasy. The truth was being fed to us in small doses, I realized.

A short, slightly overweight man stepped in front of the dark screen and gave us a strained smile.

"I expect we'll manage," he said in a booming voice. "A few basics, so you'll picture the place and it won't all be news to you. Mercury rotates in about fifty-nine Earth days. The mining complex is on the equator. As the planet reaches its closest point to the Sun, the Sun comes up over the horizon and stays there for two Earth days, then sets again. It pops up again a few days later, by Earth clocks, and moves high into the sky. Mercury is now moving toward its farthest point from the Sun again, so the Sun seems to shrink and move faster in the sky."

I had the feeling that he was trying to distract us from the real problems ahead.

"Forty-four days later along the orbit, the Sun is directly overhead. Then all this repeats itself, but backward." Someone sighed heavily behind me. "The Sun grows larger, drops down toward the west, slowing, sets, rises, and sets again. A Merk day is eighty-eight Earth days, and so is the night, almost. Its day is the same length as its year." Studdy was getting it across. Dull but accurate. I listened more closely. "It's the shape of Mercury's orbit, a flattened circle, that keeps the planet from complete tide lock with Sol, where one side would be light, the other dark. Tidal friction brakes by a factor of four, depending on where the planet is in its orbit, close in traveling fast or far out and moving slower. So it keeps one hemisphere facing the Sun when close in, but continues to rotate when far out and the gravitational bonds grow more elastic, getting more and more out of lock with the Sun. Afternoons can reach over two hundred degrees Celsius, and it can drop to minus a hundred and thirty at night. What all this means is that miners go out on the surface and work like hell for most of the night, but when the Sun rises all labor is confined to below-surface operations. Staying out, even in a suit or protective vehicle, would be the same as sunbathing in the light of billions of hydrogen-bomb explosions." He paused. "But they need the Sun to fill the solar-power collectors, to run the digging, smelting, and refining robots. There's more power than they could ever use, in fact. The various refined metals are cut into huge blocks and launched on the mass driver toward Earth Orbit. Some of you may have seen similar catapults on the Moon."

"What about the quakes!" someone shouted.

"Mercury's surface is still elastic, and the core is still shrinking. Temperature changes between night and day help trigger quakes. It can't be helped. Don't look at me that way—I'll be there too."

Linda stood up. "What about the underground quarters?"

"They're safe enough most of the time," Studdy answered. "People have been hurt or killed, but most survive. The quakes vary in intensity, and many structures are in poor repair. These people have little time to improve their dwellings, or repair them. They also have to maintain the industrial equipment, much of which is old and obsolete. And there's less power at night, when the solar collectors can't work. Industry, not housing development, gets the energy."

"But you said there's more than enough power," the boy with the white hair said. "Why aren't there power satellites beaming it in all the time?"

"That's one of the things the orbital habitat will make possible. High-orbit beamers require maintenance and relays. The present satellite collectors are low orbit and inefficient by today's standards."

"There's no reason a subsurface living complex couldn't be made safe," Linda said.

Studdy shrugged. "Maybe—but they've seen what free space habitats are, and that's what the agreement says they'll get."

"You mean they put a gun to Earth's head," someone said bitterly. I turned too late to see who it was, but later I learned that six people were going back with the *Wells*.

"Look, it's just as well. We'll have metals, and if Merk

is torn up completely for resources one day, as is likely, we won't have to worry about evicting anyone. There are lots of reasons human beings shouldn't live there."

"What about the solar research base?" Jake asked.

"It's well away from the mining sites, and from what I know they've never complained about their conditions. But the teams there are replaced fairly often."

I stood up. The matter-of-fact coldness of Studdy's presentation was beginning to rub me the wrong way. "You don't show much sympathy for these people, Mr. Studdy," I said, and stood there in the sudden silence, waiting for an answer.

"Listen, kid," Studdy said after a moment, "I volunteered same as you—" He stopped short. "Sorry—you're right—I have been cut-and-dried about it. We need to be reminded why we're here. What have you to say?"

I cleared my throat. "Only that we should think about how we're going to get along with these people. We shouldn't come on as their saviors. We're here to give them what should have been theirs a long time ago. Fast ships and robotic industrial equipment made it economical to mine Mercury, so it should have been economical to give these people a better life by now."

"You're right—we might get off on the wrong foot if we don't think why we're here. We have to get along with the miners. What's your name?"

"Joe Sorby."

"Thanks, Joe. But remember, there's something in it for us also—skills, experience, good pay."

Someone snickered behind me. I turned and tried to spot the person. "Why did you bother to come?" I asked loudly, and sat down.

Rosalie squeezed my hand. I felt a bit foolish, even though I knew I was right.

Mercury seemed to be waiting for us as we crossed its path and decelerated into a wide ellipse around the cratered ball. Captain Vinov then dropped us into a tight orbit, only a hundred miles above the surface, so the landing shuttles could use the whole planet as a shield against solar radiation when they ferried us down. The small craft were not as well insulated as the big ship, which carried lots of water in its triple hull, and they were especially vulnerable to solar flares—those bursts of radiation from the Sun's surface that could cook unprotected human flesh in seconds.

We went down in groups of twenty-five. Everyone seemed a bit glum, knowing that things were going to be very different from what we had expected. I didn't feel like a world builder at all. No one talked about the possible danger, but it was there, an undercurrent of fear in our minds.

Bernie, Ro, and I strapped in.

A fifty-foot tube of gray metal with a control cabin at

one end, a cargo bay fitted with couches for passengers, the shuttle frightened me with its smallness, thin walls, and shaky-looking bulkheads; it had seen too many years of service and couldn't be safe.

Being next to a porthole didn't make me feel any better; it was probably the weakest part of the vessel.

But the view was breathtaking as we went down into Mercury's night. The planet was mysterious in starlight. Looking carefully, I saw a faint string of diamonds leaving the surface: slugs of metal boosting toward Earth Orbit, to arrive many months later in a nearly endless train. The shuttle turned a bit and I saw where the slugs were high enough to catch the sunlight, bursting into prominence one by one, like stars being born. . . .

What am I doing here? I wondered as the descent engine fired below me. I lay pinned to my couch, overcome by doubt and the sudden sense of distance from home, from my parents, from my lost friend Morey, and all the things I had known as a boy. I was here to help, but would it help me? Did anyone care? Would anyone remember? I reached out to the cold stars and felt saddened by their silence as the shuttle touched down.

"What's that?" Ro asked.

"What?" I unstrapped and sat up. Everyone in the small hold was silent. The shuttle trembled, shuddered, and was still.

"We're just settling," I said.

"A quake maybe," Ro added.

"A small one," Bernie piped. "Probably happens all the time."

"And so do the big ones." I turned and saw it was Whitey with the big ears.

There was a metallic thud against the side of the craft.

"Loading tube," Bernie said.

We lined up in front of the airlock.

"How you feeling, Joe?" Bernie asked, smiling.

"Okay, I guess," I answered. But suddenly I was overcome with feeling for him, and I was glad that he was here to share what he knew with us and with the miners. It made me feel safer.

Rosalie went through the lock. I followed. The tube dropped at a thirty-degree angle, leading directly underground. We emerged into a large, ceramic-sealed chamber with rounded corners. Tunnels led off in four directions. The chamber filled quickly.

"Your attention!" a male voice announced with some strain.

I turned and saw a middle-sized man with black hair, combed back in the way I remembered from when I first saw him on the holo in Riverbend's square.

"I'm Robert Svoboda," he said more softly, examining us with dark-blue eyes. "Please follow me single file." He seemed a bit nervous and impatient. "There will have to be four of you to a room in many cases. We didn't expect to have to house you. Try to allow for our simpler conditions."

He turned and led the way out through the tunnel behind him. I felt a trembling in my boots. Svoboda stopped and turned his head slightly, as if something invisible were following him. Then his bearlike shape marched forward again.

I looked at the bare bulbs and heat-sealed walls as we followed him through the passage. We went through a half dozen round connecting areas. Locks slammed behind us, echoing ominously. The tunnels were always rough-hewn, sealed with heat, stained with humidity and mineral discolorations. We came to a row of doorways.

"These crank open by hand," Svoboda said. "Seven rooms. One rule. Keep your doors sealed when you're inside. A quake can cause a loss of pressure in the tunnels, but you'll still have air in the rooms."

"You'll share with us, Bernie," Ro said.

"Okay by me."

I cranked open the first door and stepped into darkness.

"Light's overhead!" Svoboda shouted as the other doors were opened. I reached up and pulled a cord. A bulb went on over the door, throwing my shadow across a stony floor. I held on to the cord, shocked at the room's simplicity.

There were three bunks; a sink-toilet-shower combination was partly concealed by a plastic curtain. Everything was clean, but much used. No sheets or blankets on the bunks, only sleeping bags.

"Well," Rosalie said, "it'll only be for a couple of weeks." She smiled at me, but I didn't react.

"I've seen worse," Bernie said.

I had never seen anything as bad. "The designs are so old. Look at that bulb—you can see the filament glowing."

"We'll get by," Ro said decisively.

Our shadows looked as if they had been painted on the floor. I felt another vibration in my boots. The bulb behind us flickered, filling the room with trembling shadows; the ventilator coughed, then resumed its steady whisper.

15 FURNACE IN THE SKY

The Sun breathed against the surface of Mercury. Collectors drank only a small portion of the pulsing flow of energy, but it was more than enough to run the planet's industry.

Rivers of metal flowed into molds, cooling during the long nights and sliding onto the automated sleds that hurled the slugs into fast unpowered orbits.

As we watched in the underground control center, slugs rose to become stars above the open-pit mines, a string reaching all the way to Earth Orbit, enough metals to refill the home planet's empty mines a thousand times over.

Any single chunk might take up to two years to reach the factories in Luna's L positions, but the forward slugs in the perpetual train arrived constantly, so it didn't matter; that's why it was so important not to break the steady flow—months, years, might go by before it could be restored. I was here with 199 others of the first wave to make sure that didn't happen, even if it meant helping people in the bargain!

Robert Svoboda had no illusions about the economic and political pressures that had brought us here, even if many of us were sympathetic to his cause; sympathy alone would not have been enough. He had been here from the start. He knew the work that had gone into the solar-power plants, launch-sled tracks, and housing, and what it all cost to keep. His degrees, skills, and experience were adapted to a life here. His son and wife were here. Many of the miners had spent half their lives here, laboring like some Hephaestian horde to feed Earth's needs.

Svoboda's aim was to improve the lives of the ten thousand people on Mercury. To them it seemed that the rest of the solar system was building paradises. There were certainly enough resources to build paradises, so why shouldn't they have one too? They shipped enough metals for a thousand habitats, so they deserved an oasis in the sea of solar radiation, away from the rock, dust, and quakes. They were willing to work here, even raise families—I came to understand why later—if they could feel reasonably safe. One of the first things Svoboda showed us were the sealed tunnels that served as tombs for the miners trapped by the quake of '28.

After only a few days, many of us began to pick up the miners' attitudes. Rosalie and I began to hate the buried hovels. Who cared about the motives of Earth in sending us here! There was going to be something better before we were done.

The real problem of building a large habitat in orbit around Mercury, once the political decision had been made, was not in the basic work. A large slug could have been blown up into an empty shell years ago, if the miners had diverted the work force and slowed up deliveries to Earth. Even the shielding was pretty routine engineering. The difficulty was in getting the skilled environmentalists to shape the ecology within the shell, the life-support systems that would be reliable and pleasing. It was an art to make an inner surface look like the out of doors. The number of specialists was limited, and they were expensive, even if they could be convinced to come to Mercury for the long time needed to do the job right. I understood the bitterness of the Mercurians, and why Earth Authority was now applying money and personal pressures to gather the talent. Not everyone could be expected to come here because they thought it was the right thing to do; the problem had to be blitzed before it got completely out of hand, whatever the dangers. Nothing else was possible at this late date.

But a rushed approach to the interior work would risk repeating the failure of the first L-5 colony, which had become a barren cylinder of concrete townhouses—cramped, ugly, and inefficient. It was now an industrial warehouse. Only skilled workers could build an easily maintainable and improvable habitat, and these people were not to be had until the Asteroids had come to Mercury's help. By providing the empty husk of the asteroid, and by forcing Earth to make good on an old promise, the Asteroids had confirmed a bond with Mercury. Building up the insides would still require a large force, but not as large as would have been needed to start from scratch. Ro and I belonged to the easily re-cruited, to those who would be trained on the job, not to the highly paid elite; only my association with Bernie gave me a bit of prestige.

I wondered about myself. Events not of my making had been the occasion for decisions I might never have thought of making. But now that I was seeing the life of Mercury close up, and feeling my own life in danger, I knew that the anger I had felt on Bernal was justified. It was not enough to know and understand; one had to act, especially when given the chance.

Svoboda surprised many of us. He could have left years ago, it seemed to us, and found a better position anywhere in Sunspace, but he was determined to make things better here. He made me feel the same way; after all, I was going to be here only a short time, so how could I do less? I think he noticed these feelings in many of us, despite the politics that had sent us here, and that helped.

There wasn't much to do while we waited for the asteroid. Svoboda gave us a tour of the underground town during the first few days.

There were three underground villages, covering some thirty square miles. Each had a large central meeting chamber, where people gathered to dance, sing, or watch programs from Earth. Solar activity made watching programs difficult at times, despite the relay satellites, even when both planets were on the same side of the Sun. The tunnels ran for hundreds of miles, and more were being cut as space was needed.

"I want you all to be very careful," Svoboda said toward the end of his tour. "If anyone is injured severely, or develops a major disease, we can't put you in suspended animation—we just don't have the equipment to hold life. If we can't treat it, you die."

We were all a bit shocked at this. He might just as well have told us that there weren't any first-aid kits, or that we could die of a simple infection.

"How did your community grow?" I asked. "From what I know it wasn't supposed to be permanent."

He smiled. "People married. Others sent for their loved ones, had kids. There was no plan. Earth Authority administrators ran us on a rotational basis, but in time that was left to us. It was too hard for ambitious career types, who came and left as soon as they could."

"So you run yourselves?"

"Almost, but the strings are still there—long, but we

feel them. How could all this happen? I can see the question in your faces. Well, toward the end of the last century people finally understood that to have a humane culture on Earth they would have to go out into space. But they began to take for granted those who went out to run their industry and get their resources for them. Not all problems are material; some are organizational, political, helping injustice exist in the midst of plenty."

"People never learn," I said.

"They do, individually, but societies forget. It was thought that Sunspacers would take care of themselves in everything. Until people live forever, each generation will have to learn things fresh."

"There's tradition, institutions, history," Ro said.

"But reminders are needed." He looked over his shoulder at the big screen, then back at our group. "Can you all find your own way? I have some work to do."

"I think we can," I said.

"Oh—here's my son, Bob. He'll go with you."

Robert Svoboda, Jr., looked like his father—thinner and slightly taller, but with the same black hair and pale-blue eyes. He had come to the common area a few times, and I had liked him immediately, though he seemed to worship his father too much.

We followed him out from the control center.

* * *

The miners grew very busy as the Sun climbed to its noon position; this was the time of maximum energy reception, use, and storage.

While the great robots ripped ore from the pits, while nuclear charges were set to open still more holes, while people struggled to repair aging equipment in the underground garages, and while the sluices ran rivers of liquid metals into molds, the support army prepared food, cleaned quarters, nursed the injured, kept records, and planned shifts. Children were being raised and educated at the same time. Many were about my age. Many seemed terrified that they would never finish school—that the next quake would stop them. The whole society was at war with time and the Sun, hurrying to mine and smelt as much metal as possible during the three months of light.

I felt guilty eating, sleeping, and waiting nervously while all this work was going on. A few jokes were made about us; some of the people our age were openly hostile; but grudgingly the idea took hold that we were being saved for other work. Mercury's gravity, only about thirty-nine percent of Earth's, made us much stronger, though we had to keep up our muscles with daily exercise and take some care in how we moved around.

People live longer on lower-g worlds like the Moon and Mars. Fighting Earth's gravity wears out your muscles, deforms your stomach and gives you backaches. Your heart lifts tons of blood through endless miles.

Here that strain was reduced by sixty-one percent, and a human being could clear a hundred even without medical help, if the quakes didn't get him first.

"They hope so much," Ro said one day.

We spent a lot of time in the common areas, playing cards and listening to music, or just talking, but it was all just a way of waiting. I tried to study some of the required technical material, but the delay and the constant thought of danger were getting to me.

Bernie tried to stay away from the room, to give Ro and me some privacy, and that was a relief; but both of us were beginning to feel oppressed, closed in. The miners felt this way all the time, I told myself, but it didn't help.

"It won't be much longer," Ro said one afternoon. "The asteroid has been in sight for days now."

I kissed her for a long time.

"Miss zero-g?" she asked softly.

"Sure." I got out of bed and put on my coveralls and boots.

"What is it, Joe?"

"Nothing." I was beginning to lose the sense of being myself again. "We may be here much longer than we expected. It's beginning to sink in, I guess."

"We decided to come," she said firmly.

"If we could just get started—instead of all this waiting." The light flickered as I zipped up my boots.

"It won't be long now."

I looked at her. "It's dangerous here—some of us might never see home again. Did you see how many injured they treat in the hospital?" I had a sudden vision of Ro lying there with every bone in her body broken.

"I've spent time with the patients too," she answered. "Only a few were really bad, and not from quakes—not recently anyway."

"You heard, didn't you?" I insisted. "They can't freeze anyone. If it's a bad injury you don't have a chance. What if it were me? Or you? It's ten days back to Earth, when you can get a ship!"

"I know," she said in a low voice. "I'm afraid, too."

I sat down on the bed and we held hands, as if afraid to let go. I had the feeling that I was about to fall apart, and the pieces wouldn't recognize each other. Ro was looking at me very carefully as she lay warm and soft in the sleeping bag. We were quiet for what seemed a long time.

"There's always a bit of you I can't see," she said finally. "I know that you love me, you're helpful and caring about people, and you work when you think the job is worth doing. But there is always a part of you that you hold back. Oh, I don't mind, but someday I hope you'll tell me about it."

She was right. There was always a part of me that longed for the clean, cold beauty of the stars. I still wasn't so sure that being a human being was so great. Maybe

214

I wanted more than the universe had to give? That's
what Morey and I still had in common—he wanted to
be more than a human being, and in my own way I still
wanted the same thing, to be able to say that this wasn't
all I was, that there could be more, that there had to be
more. I had learned one thing already—the miners were
in a bad situation, but their response was superhuman.
If they could do it, then so could I.

There was a loud knock on the door. I tensed, fearing
an emergency of some kind.

"Who is it?" I asked loudly.

"Bob Svoboda," a muffled voice replied.

I went to the door and cranked it open a crack. Bob
smiled at me. "I came to invite the three of you to dinner
at our place."

"Uh, sure," I said clumsily.

"At eight. My family would very much like to have
you. Sorry to disturb you." He smiled and moved away.

"Why us?" Ro asked as I cranked the door shut.

"Who knows. It'll be a change."

"Maybe we were picked at random," she said.

The lights flickered a lot, leaving us in darkness three
times as we made our way toward the Svoboda apartment. Finally, we came to a massive door at the end of
a long tunnel in the north village.

"Looks like the entrance to a leader's lair," Ro said.

"Watch it." Bernie pointed to a crack in the rock floor.

We stepped over the break and stood before the door. The knocker was a chunk of ore on a chain. I struck twice.

"Come in, come in," Bob said as the door slid open.

We filed past him into a large living area, onto a large green rug that covered the center of the red tile floor.

"My parents will be out in a minute."

Ro and I sat down in the chairs facing the sofa. Bernie lowered himself into the middle of the sofa and bobbed for a moment before settling. Moving around in low-g took some care until you got used to it, especially when dealing with air-filled furniture.

"Dinner will be a bit late," Bob said. "We all got home late."

The green plastic of the furniture, I noticed, did not match the rug. Cracks marred the ceiling and walls. There were some flat pictures on the end table by my chair—shots of a dark-haired girl of about seven, and an older, dark-haired boy.

"My brother and sister," Bob said. "Alexei and Liza-veta died three years ago in a quake. A wall in the day care caved in. Most of the kids survived. They found one of the babies under Liza. She'd protected him with her body."

I didn't know what to say. Bernie swallowed hard. A sad look came into Ro's eyes.

Bob made a face. "So—when do you think we'll move into the habitat?"

"We'll know better," Bernie said, "when we get the full force working inside the rock shell."

Bob was looking at me. He seemed nervous about the way I was examining the room. "It's all I've heard about since I was a kid."

"You were born here?" Ro asked.

"In the hospital."

"And you've never been away?" I asked.

He shrugged. "Maybe I'll go to college on Luna when the habitat is ready." He gave me a panicky look. "I know that's a bit late, but *you're* taking time off to work here. As long as I get a chance to learn."

Robert and Eleanor Svoboda came into the room. The Mercurian leader looked straight at me, as if trying to learn more about me.

Eleanor was a tall, thin woman with short, curly brown hair. She looked at us in turn and smiled. She seemed tired, but there was strength in her brown eyes.

"I've wanted to meet as many of your group as possible," Robert Svoboda said, "while you still have time."

There was an awkward silence.

"Thank you for inviting us," Ro said.

We stood up and followed the Svobodas through an arch. As we sat down at the table, Bob appeared in the archway from the kitchen, wheeling in the soup. We took our bowls from the cart as he went around.

"Um—good," Ro said. "Not like any mushroom soup I've tasted."

"There's bean curd in it," Bob said as he sat down between his parents. "I've made it since I was a kid." He rolled his eyes.

I happened to like the mushroom dishes I had tasted on Merk, but then I usually didn't eat them all the time, either. Because it was easy to grow them here in parts of the dark tunnels, mushrooms were plentiful and seemed to turn up in almost everything I ate.

"I'm glad you like it," Mrs. Svoboda said, smiling.

"It's very fine, Mrs. Svoboda," I said, knowing that I wouldn't want to have her angry at me for anything.

"Please," she said, "call us Robert and Eleanor. Now— you're Joe, Rosalie, and Bernard."

"Call me Bernie."

"I hope the delay hasn't been too boring," Robert Svoboda said from the head of the table. "I'm aware that there has been some bad feeling—"

"We're anxious to work," I said.

Bob wheeled out our empty bowls and breezed back with the main course. We took our plates as he went around. I looked at what seemed to be a piece of meat with mushroom gravy, green beans, and a potato. My feet trembled as I took a bite.

Robert Svoboda looked up, his face a hard mask.

He stared right through me. I tensed. Then his face softened as quickly as it had gone rigid. He ran his fingers back through his hair and sighed.

We were silent.

"Well?" he asked harshly.

"Is there anything we should do if one comes?" I asked.

"We're on a bad fault, Joe. The big danger is in loss of pressure and cave-in." A distant look came into his eyes. "It didn't seem so bad in the early years, but it got worse."

"And we got used to worse," Eleanor added.

I looked at her and realized that she had seen people die. When she looked at her son, she saw that her future was still being held hostage. I imagined living here with Ro all these years, and it frightened me.

"Things will be better," Eleanor said nervously, trying to sound cheerful. "Bob, the wine."

Bob almost tripped as he went out to the kitchen. On Earth he would not have been able to right himself and catch the chair so quickly; there were some advantages to lower g.

"You're the third group we've had to dinner," Eleanor said, sounding more in control of herself.

"What do you think of us?" Ro asked, and my stomach jumped.

"You're nice people to leave your schooling. I hope you don't lose too much time."

Bob brought back a large green bottle and poured out full glasses for everyone. The white liquid trembled slightly in my goblet. Robert Svoboda was staring intently at his glass. Bob put the bottle on the table and sat down.

Robert Svoboda raised his glass. "I want to thank you personally, even if you have doubts about being here. You're not likely to get any medals from Earth Authority."

We sipped.

"The grapes grow well here," Eleanor said.

Bob saw his chance. "We sure have enough sun!"

We laughed and sipped some more.

"Where are you from, Joe?" Robert Svoboda asked.

"New York City."

He held back a laugh. "Now I know you're not used to our quarters. Must seem like jail cells. How about you, Rosalie, Bernie?"

"I'm from Bernal," Ro said.

"Same here," Bernie added.

"He helped build the place," I said.

Svoboda's eyebrows went up. "Bernal functions admirably. I visited once. . . . It seems so long ago now." Eleanor gazed at him with concern.

Bob rolled out tea and coffee after dinner. We took

our cups and followed Eleanor out into the living room, where we reclaimed our seats. Bob sat cross-legged on the floor. His parents sat on some shabby black cushions. I wondered how many people had died on Mercury, but was afraid to ask.

Eleanor smiled at me, and I saw how beautiful she was, how even more beautiful she had been.

"What were you studying, Joe?" she asked.

"Physics—I thought."

"You're not sure?"

I sipped my tea. "Maybe later, I don't know."

"Rosalie, what interests you, besides Joe?"

I looked at her. She was blushing.

"There are a number of things I might want to do."

Robert Svoboda's brooding concern filled the room, pressing in around us. These people had almost forgotten how to relax. They might have left a long time ago and found a better life, but there were too many dead for the Svobodas to leave. The Svobodas carried Mercury on their shoulders.

"How many of your people do you think will stay after the habitat is built?" Bernie asked.

Robert looked surprised. "This is their home—a whole generation has grown up here. That may be hard for some people to understand, but it's always been true. People have lived in deserts and on frozen tundra—it's actually easier than that here." A strangeness came into his eyes, as if he were peering through the rock. "There is beauty in living here, in stealing Mercury's insides while the big Sun stands watch. A habitat will take off the rough edges. Then maybe more people will immigrate here, and those here will feel better about staying."

"How big will the habitat be?" Bob asked. I could see that he just couldn't wait.

"The asteroid is maybe twelve kilometers long," Bernie said. "That should take over a hundred thousand people in time."

Hope and wonder danced in Bob's eyes, and right there I knew that it would all be worth it.

"I've always wanted a house," Eleanor said, "with sky and clouds and sunlight coming in through the windows. . . ."

"The old mass driver," Bernie continued, "will be replaced by the gravitational catapult. You'll be able to shove slugs into faster orbits toward Earth. And the string of solar-power satellites will relay energy to Mercury's surface even when the sun is down, so you'll have full industrial capacity all the time."

Svoboda said, "Some of my men suspect they'll only have to work harder."

"I don't think so," Bernie replied.

I heard a high-pitched whine. Svoboda turned his head suddenly. "I'm being called. Excuse me." He stood up and left the room.

Eleanor motioned to her son. "Maybe you'd like to take our guests to the Center?"

"Uh—maybe later," Bob said. I guessed he wanted us to himself for a while. "What's it like on Earth, Joe?"

I told him about open skies, colorful sunsets, ocean waves, winds and rainstorms, tall cities and crowds. "You'll see it yourself one day," I finished, not thinking about what I was saying.

He shook his head. "It would be hard. Remember, I was born here, my muscles grew up here. I'd have to wear walking bones to brace me in the higher gravity. Maybe I could adjust—I've always exercised. I can go to the Moon, Mars, the Asteroids, maybe even Bernal, which isn't a full g anyway, and much lower in places."

I felt sorry for him, as if he were crippled. Lucky for him there were good schools on places besides Earth. On the Moon he'd have to exercise to keep up his Mercury muscles in the one-sixth gravity. I'd never thought too much about it, but it was an important problem.

"That's another reason we need the habitat," Eleanor said, "so we can have the choice of gradually increasing the g-spin at which our children are born, so future generations won't be cut off from Earth. Many of our people are now too old to ever go back."

"That may take a long time," I said.

"It may never happen," Eleanor continued, "if enough

of us decide against it. It's how it happened in the first place that's shameful."

"People were promised regular trips back," Bob said. "Some go now, but only because the ships have grown faster. In the old days people traveled back and forth in pods attached to a slug. It took months in zero-g. Not many went."

"The Asteroid settlers," Eleanor continued, "keep their habitats at two thirds Earth gravity, so they can go anywhere, while we can go only to the low-g places in the solar system. That was the point with those serving life sentences, to trap them here, but others were caught and are now too bitter and too weak to go even if they could."

"That's terrible," I said, as the full implications sank in. Earth had done this, but I felt as if I had done it myself. The habitat had to be built as quickly as possible.

Eleanor smiled at my sense of outrage. "It'll be easier on future generations. It's hardest on those who remember Earth."

"It's not so bad," Bob said. "People do live longer in low-g, and they don't have back trouble, without all the medical fix-up you have to go through on Earth."

"Why did people have children," Rosalie asked, "if they knew they'd be trapped?"

Eleanor grimaced. "They said to go ahead—raise families, you'll have your habitat."

"They treated us *all* like convicts," Robert Svoboda said as he came back and sat down next to his wife. "Problems in the control room. The foreman is sick."

"Where are you from, Eleanor?" Ro asked.

"Virginia. I was in my teens when Robert and I left."

Svoboda took her hand. "We'll visit. We can get in shape, you'll see. Our muscles will remember."

Her face was calm, but I felt angry for her.

"Bob," Eleanor said, "the Community Center."

We all stood up. Eleanor was smiling faintly at me. Robert looked as if he had just gotten his second wind, and I knew he was going to visit the control room.

"Thank you for coming," Eleanor said.

"Care to come with me, Bernie?" Svoboda asked.

"Thanks—but I've got to get some sleep."

Bob led us to the door. "I usually go down to the Center dance anyway." He turned the crank.

We stepped out and over the crack. Ro and I held hands as we followed him.

"Have a good time," Bernie said at the first branching, sounding a bit lonely.

"Good night, Bernie!" I called after him as he disappeared into the tunnel at our left.

16 DANCING

Two massive doors stood at the end of the passageway. One was cranked partly open, spilling yellow light into the rocky tunnel. Music mingled with voices and laughter.

The Community Center had always been full of kids when I'd looked in, but Ro and I had been shy about going in uninvited. Most of us kept to the common areas near our quarters. Many of the Merk kids were not as polite as their parents, we had noticed, but I couldn't blame them; Mercury had good reason to dislike Earth, without our making it look as if we had come to take over. The Merk kids *needed* to feel superior to us, at least for a while. It would be easier going in with Bob Svoboda.

The chamber was a fused upside-down bowl, at least seven meters high at the center and sixty meters across. Dancers surrounded the screen platform—at least a hundred couples spinning, rubbing, and jerk jumping to the percussion. The flat screen, not a three-dee holo, was picking up music and dance from a New York station, delayed by the six minutes or so it took the signal to reach Mercury at light speed, not counting relay time. There was a sharp contrast between the well-dressed New York kids on the screen and the coverall drabness of the Mercurians.

I spotted Linda and Jake. Her hair was loose and flying in all directions. He seemed to be doing his best not to become airborne. We had all tried hard not to show off by doing things the Mercurians could not—like jumping high into the air. It would be easy for us to win fights with Merk kids, given our stronger Earth muscles. I had been careful not to use my full strength when moving around. The Merk girls looked at us with some interest, which annoyed their boyfriends.

"Hey!" someone shouted. "Let's see you go up real high!"

The dancers made a circle around Linda and Jake.

"Come on—do it!"

Jake looked around, and jumped.

"You can do better than that!" the same voice shouted.

The crowd hooted. I sensed both hostility and interest in their demand.

Jake motioned for Linda not to do it, but she went up high, turned over, and landed in a group of people, toppling them to the floor.

Everyone laughed.

"Don't worry—they'll be here long enough to weaken!"

A boy I didn't know shot up higher, and landed on a couple.

"I've sprained my ankle!" the girl complained, unable to get to her feet. Her boyfriend did not look amused. I caught his eye and he glared at me.

"How's she going to work?" he demanded.

I felt bad.

"They're not so tough," another boy said, giving Jake a shove from behind. Someone cursed. Jake stumbled toward me and I caught him.

"Calm down!" a voice boomed over the screen's public address system, but it was too late.

A fair fight wouldn't have been possible, despite our Earth muscles; there were only eleven of us in the hall. The crowd booed as the music dropped to a whisper and we were rushed from all sides. People fell to the floor, punching and clawing, tearing at each other's clothes. Ro and I retreated through a sudden hole in the circle. A short, stocky girl grabbed Linda by the hair. Jake was being pummeled on the floor by three boys. The Merks were doing very well, but I was afraid that someone would get seriously hurt.

The crowd pressed in closer, cheering. I saw a familiar New York caster on the screen, speaking very low. His blindness to what was going on below him seemed comic.

A loud whistle shot through my ears as police invaded

the hall. It was obvious that they had been watching the situation closely. Six green-uniformed cops penetrated the crowd and began to untie the knot of kids on the floor.

"Okay!" shouted one of the cops. His voice went through his handset and boomed through the screen speakers. "All earthies out of the hall!"

One of the other cops glared at me. Bob smiled and I saw a bit of his parents in his features.

"It was our fault," I said loudly. "Let's go."

Linda, Kik, Jake and the six others grouped around Ro and me. We turned and led the way out.

"That was really dumb," I whispered to Ro.

"Sure was," she said, looking exasperated.

A cop cranked the door open all the way, and we went out into the tunnel.

I heard a deep growl, as if some beast were creeping toward us from somewhere ahead. We stopped, but nothing showed itself. It was invisible, I thought stupidly as the lights flickered.

"What's that?" Kik asked behind me.

I peered ahead in the fluttering light. A cloud of fine dust was creeping toward us across the floor.

"Tremor," I said, taking a few steps forward.

"Joe . . ." Ro started to say as the floor lifted, throwing me back. We clutched at each other and staggered to one side, hitting the wall with our shoulders.

Old Merk danced for us.

The tunnel floor buckled and split. Ro and I were on all fours, tasting dust.

"Back inside!" I shouted as I raised myself on shaky legs.

A crack opened near the doors and cut down the tunnel like slow black lightning. We jumped to avoid it.

The lights wavered. I saw Kik stumble, fall in slowly between blinks, and disappear. Ro and I were on opposite sides as the crack passed us, veered, and split the wall.

"Kik!" Linda cried, unsteady at the edge.

"Get back!" I shouted, afraid that the fault would widen.

"Kik!" she called. "Kik!"

Jake grabbed her.

"Aaaaaaaaaaaaa!" she wailed, struggling. It looked as if she would pull Jake in with her.

"Back into the hall!" I shouted again.

Ro and I made our way back, staring at the fault between us. The others were at the door, but Linda still squirmed in Jake's arms.

"Let me go, let me go!"

Jake hauled her back. "He's gone—we've got to get back—try to understand what I'm saying." She broke free and dropped to her knees. Jake tried to pull her back by one arm.

"No! No! I can see him!"

"Help me," Jake said as I reached them. Ro hesitated at the door.

"Get inside," I called to her and grabbed Linda's other arm.

"He's hanging there," she insisted, "I can see him." She was very strong. "I can see him—please look!"

I peered down and she stopped wriggling. "Can't see a thing," I said, coughing from the dust.

"Don't let go," Jake whispered.

Linda looked up at me. "Joe! Look hard—I can see him, please!"

I strained to see into the gloom. There was a body hanging some five meters below us. "Jake, he's there."

"Looks like a shadow."

"Let me go!" Linda shrieked, twisting her arms. "Let me go!"

"I'll go," Jake said, and let go her hand.

I knelt next to Linda and we watched him climb down. Linda's arm was limp in my hand.

Merk trembled.

"Inside!" a cop shouted. "Got to close these doors."

"Injured person," I called back.

"It's you or all those in here, son." Loss of air pressure in the tunnel might come at any moment, I realized.

"Linda," I said, tugging her arm as I stood up.

"You go," she said, pulling free of me.

I heard the door closing.

"Jake—they're locking us out!"

"Coming!"

"Kik!" Linda shouted.

"He's gone," Jake called more softly.

The lights went out. I turned and saw that the door was three quarters closed.

"Kik! Bring him up—Jake do you hear me?"

"Head's caved in where he hit," Jake said. "His neck is broken and he's stuck on some sharp rocks. No breathing at all. Get going, both of you! Can't see. Got to feel my way up." His voice broke and I remembered that they had been friends.

"Let's go, Linda." My eyes were adjusting to the light still coming through the open door.

She let me pull her up. "You bastards—you'll leave him there," she mumbled through her tears.

The cop cursed as the crank jammed.

Even if there had been time for Jake and me to bring up the body, Kik was too damaged for freezing, even if we'd had the facilities, which we did not.

Jake climbed up over the edge. We took Linda by the arms and led her to the door.

"Give me a hand," the cop said as we pushed her inside.

The three of us worked the crank. It turned slowly and I thought it might break, but finally the doors closed—just as the ground trembled again.

"What now?" I asked. Linda was on the floor nearby, crying softly.

"We wait for help," the cop said, looking at me with gray eyes. He couldn't have been more than five years older than me. His ruddy face was flushed from effort. Sweat ran down from under his cap as he wiped his forehead with a sleeve.

"Is that likely?" Jake asked.

The cop nodded. "The whole warren couldn't have been affected."

We turned and walked to the platform. Most of the kids were sitting on the floor. Bob was on the platform with the other cops, trying to get through on the intercom.

"Cable's gone," he said when he saw me. "At least from here out. It's happened before. They'll come and get us, eventually."

Rosalie was suddenly next to me. "How long?" she asked.

Bob shrugged. "Depends on the damage."

"But what do you think?" I asked.

"Don't worry—the Control Center can survive anything."

I looked around at the kids on the floor. They looked patient, resigned; they'd gone through this before. Many of them, I realized, had probably lost friends and relatives. Kik was gone, I reminded myself. We hadn't been

exactly friends, but I had come to like him from a distance.

"We'll know soon enough," Bob added. His parents
might be dead or injured, for all he knew. "Find a com-
fortable spot," he said confidently. "Air seems to be coming in well enough. We'll have to wait."

I noticed the way everyone looked at him. He was
Robert Svoboda's son, after all. I wondered what good
that would do us if nothing could be done.

Jake was kneeling by Linda. He kissed her cheek and
put his arm around her. I realized how close he had
come to dying; the fissure might have closed at any moment, or another shock might have thrown him deeper.
All three of us might have died if the tunnel had de-
compressed—but Linda, I realized with a sudden sick
feeling, had now lost all the family she had left.

Ro and I climbed up and sat on the edge of the platform. A few faces glanced up at us from time to time.
Linda seemed to grow calmer as Jake held her. They
seemed very alone on the open floor, away from the
crowd around the platform. . . .

I was in a kind of shock myself, I suppose, as the
situation sank into my mind. The universe is a one-way
street; you can't always know what it's going to do to
you, and you can't do all that much back. We've learned
a lot, and we're going to know a lot more before the
Sun dies—but what was happening here on Mercury
was the result of what we had done to ourselves; many

people had seen it coming—but why is it that some see and others don't? I was a bit frightened, and one of us had died, but the Mercurians had been living with this kind of danger for decades.

The lights went out. A cry of surprise passed through the crowd. Ro's hand slipped into mine. She squeezed hard and I squeezed back. It seemed strange to be so near the Sun and in total darkness—yet something in me needed to be here, so far from home, in the blackness, before I could become myself. That was the part of me that Ro had complained about not being able to see. We all have it, I suppose, the mysterious bit of ourselves that we feel but don't often understand. The conscious part of us is not all there is. Self-conscious reason is the new kid on the block, evolution's jewel—but within us still live the impulses of fish and reptile, unthinking hunger and hatred, to which darkness and danger give a home.

"We're never gonna get out," a boyish voice said.

"Who's *that*?" a girl asked disgustedly.

"One of yours," Bob whispered. "Sounds like he may panic. Do you know him?"

"No."

"Shut up!" the same girl shouted.

"That's one of ours," Bob said.

"Can't we do anything?" the plaintive voice asked. My stomach swam at the sound.

"Eat your way out!"

"Come on, you two," another girl said.

"Leave him alone," a husky female voice answered.

"He had it too good on Earth. Serves him right!"

"Earth! That's where you have to wear a strap to keep your balls from dragging on the ground!"

"Boobs too!"

There was some laughter. It was only human to be resentful, I thought bitterly. *Only human.* Why weren't people better inside as time went on?

"Cut it out!" Jake shouted from near the doors. "Insult us when the lights are on."

"Just keep yapping, I'll find you."

"Okay," Bob said. "Stay put—or you'll have to deal with me later."

"That goes for me too," the cop said from somewhere on my right.

"Who are you?"

A light flashed onto a face. "Sergeant Black. There's five of us in here, so behave." I recognized the ruddy complexion.

"Oooooooooh!"

Everyone laughed.

"I know that's you, Ted," Sergeant Black said.

"Big deal," a girl's nasal monotone replied.

"Helen Wodka? I can tell it's you."

"Whattyaa—a voice printer? She's not even here, stupid."

"Cops could help out with work instead of following us around all week."

"Hey kid—I work two shifts!"

"Crawl away!" Miss Nasal shouted.

"Why do you have it in for me?" Black demanded.

"Get lost!"

Someone laughed nervously. The darkness was taking away the normal walls between people; you could say what you wanted. The fun of the evening was gone, and nothing could be done against old Merk, but cops and strangers were easy targets.

I had a sudden vision of a long chain of *because*s locking together to trap Ro and me here. Political delays in giving the aid owed to Mercury were going to cost even more lives—including mine and Ro's. The past had sealed us into this hall. I waited for someone to start picking on earthies in earnest, but it didn't happen.

We listened to each other's breathing and to the sound of the ventilator. My eyes were wide open, searching the dark for a spot of light. I began to see patterns of brightness in the blackness. Kaleidoscope universes burst and re-formed, one creation after another dying in my brain. . . .

"Black—are you there?"

"I'm here, Helen."

"Sorry, Black."

"Me too," Ted added.

A few more apologies whispered through the hall.

I heard a click—a lighter blossomed and I saw our shadows sitting on the walls. The darkness closed in again, and after a few moments I saw the red ember of a cigarette hanging in space.

Black speared the offender with his flashlight beam. "Put it out—our air might not last." The beam died before I could see the smoker. The red spot dropped and died as Black's words sank in.

"There must be something we can do!" Linda cried.

"What do you suggest?" Black asked calmly, and it seemed to me that these people were so beaten down that they didn't want to do anything. Suddenly I wanted to run time back, so that Kik would come floating out of the abyss, alive and whole, even if it meant that we would have to live backward from then on.

Linda's voice had made me edgy. I wanted to move around, fight back. It couldn't be very serious, I told myself, if Bob and the cops were so calm. It was just a minor inconvenience. The lights would go on in a moment and the dance would start up again. But working with Bernie had taught me to be suspicious; anything that could go wrong would go wrong.

"Listen," Bob said. "Everyone be quiet."

I heard only breathing. Ro squeezed my hand and we both knew what had happened.

"We're not getting any air," Bob said in a sinking voice. "Can't hear the ventilator. . . ."

I tensed.

"Must be blocked," Helen said.

"Don't move around—relax," Black said. "We'll make it last. This is a big hall."

But there are a lot of us, I thought.

"Can we tell if there's air in the tunnel without opening the doors?" Jake asked.

"No," Black replied. "It may be blocked even if there's air."

"Can't we crack it a bit and listen for a hiss?" a boy asked, and again I realized how ancient much of the technology here was—there should have been pressure sensors on the doors, so you could tell if there was air on the other side, or what you would be breathing.

"Don't talk stupid," Helen Wodka said. "Why risk a stuck door when all we have to do is wait. A small leak will kill us sooner if we can't close the door, if we're not sucked out into a vacuum first."

"We can't touch the door," Black added.

"How long can we breathe?" I asked, knowing it would be an unwelcome question.

"Depends on how much we use."

"You mean we can go quietly, lying around," the sad-voiced boy said bitterly.

"No more talk like that," Black answered firmly.

I put my arm around Ro's waist and held her tightly.

"What if the rest of the warrens got clobbered?" Jake asked.

I heard Bob take a deep breath.

"Leave some for the rest of us," a girl's voice said.

"Unlikely," Bob replied. "It's never happened—they'll get us out." He was sounding less convincing.

"There's got to be *something* we can do," Linda said again, more calmly. Again I felt the pressure to act, even though I wasn't feeling much like Tarzan.

"Bob," I said loudly, "—are the ventilation shafts large enough to crawl through?"

"Sure," he answered, "but there's probably nowhere to go. The one leading out of here is probably crushed. You might not be able to breathe."

"We should explore," I said. "We can do that much."

"It's worth a try," Black said. "We might restore air-flow if the blockage is nearby."

"I'll go," Jake and I said at the same time.

"Both of you go," Bob said. "The buddy system is safer."

Someone stumbled toward the platform. A flashlight blinked on, throwing the beam into the high vault of the hall. "Here," Black said, reaching up to me, "take my light."

"We need another," Bob called.

I took the light and cast the beam across the crowd. One of the cops handed his over at the edge of the seated crowd; the flashlight passed from hand to hand until it reached Jake.

"The shaft is behind us," Bob said.

"Don't lose those lights," Black said.

I kissed Rosalie. "If you die I'll kill you," she whispered.

"Let's go, pal," Jake said.

We turned our beams onto the wall behind the platform, and found the grill.

"About four meters up," Jake said.

"Roll the platform over," Bob said. "It's on coasters."

A dozen people pushed the stage up against the wall.

"Get on my shoulders," Jake said.

I put the flashlight in my chest pocket, so the beam would shine upward, and climbed onto Jake's shoulders. The grating felt solid when I pulled on it.

"Doesn't move even a little." Then I jerked harder and it came loose."Look out." I dropped it near the wall and heard the clatter after the slow fall.

Jake boosted me into the shaft, where I turned around carefully and looked out over the hall. Dark lumps sat in the center. Shadowed faces peered up at me in the faint light.

"Coming up!" Jake called.

"Come ahead!" I backed into the shaft.

Jake's shape appeared in the opening and pulled itself in. I caught his face in my beam for a moment. He coughed and crawled toward me.

"We're in!" he shouted over his shoulder.

"Be careful," Black answered.

I turned and crawled ahead with the light in my left hand. There was no movement of air in the pipe.

"It branches here," I called out after thirty meters. Shining the light to the right, I saw that the passage went on for a few meters and came to another grating. "What's next to the auditorium?"

I waited as Jake relayed my question. "Bob says go ahead," he shouted back. "It's the police station."

I crawled to the grating. "It's blocked with debris on the other side—cave-in!" I backed away. "I'm going to try the left-hand pipe."

My light flickered as I slid forward. I turned it off.

"Can't see your light!"

"Saving it!"

The dusty air was getting harder to breathe. I crawled for what seemed an hour, scraping my knees and coughing.

Finally I stopped and flicked on my beam.

And froze.

"The pipe's crushed!" I shouted, choking. It was like a bent straw. I struggled to control my coughing.

"Are you okay?"

"Yes!" I wished he would shut up.

"What?"

"I'm fine!"

I killed my light, turned, and started back, wondering how many of us would die. Help would reach us

—but did anyone know we were running out of air? I thought of my life on Earth and Bernal. How small my problems there now seemed. I was drenched in sweat. There was less dust but the air was beginning to taste bad.

"Joe!"

"Coming," I croaked with a dry throat.

You never really believe you're ever going to die. When you imagine it, you stand outside yourself, watching yourself go, and you're still *there* when it's over, watching from some fabulous beyond. . . .

I heard breathing.

"Jake?"

His light went on. His face seemed old and afraid suddenly. "What's wrong, Joe?"

"Gotta rest." I lay down and put my head on my arms. "There's no way out. . . ."

"Then we'll just have to last."

"I guess. . . ."

My eyes were wide open in the dark, and it seemed strange to be lying there, doing nothing. I forced myself up on all fours.

"We'd better get back," Jake said.

He retreated to the opening, left his light for me to see by, and lowered himself over the edge until he was hanging by both hands. I came forward, picked up his flashlight and shone it down on the platform. Jake dropped slowly onto both feet.

"Catch." The flashlight fell like a dying star into his hands. I crawled over the edge, held, then dropped. Hands steadied me as I came down.

The air tasted better. I saw Ro's face. She was biting her lips.

"We'll have to take it easy until help arrives," Jake said. "Joe says both ways are blocked."

I sat down against the wall. Ro sat down next to me.

"What's going on?" someone asked from the floor.

Silence.

"Well?" the same male voice asked. "What have you big shots come up with?"

"Didn't you hear!" Jake snapped. "We'll have to wait."

I heard murmuring and cursing.

"There's gotta be something . . ."

"Ted—is that you?" Bob asked.

"Yeah, I'm not a lump yet."

"We'll use less air," Bob said.

"And when that's gone," Ted continued, "we'll have to open the doors. We won't have anything to lose then—and who knows, it might be all right out there."

Again, there was a nervous silence.

"We should have been living in a habitat by now," Helen Wodka said. "What took you people so long? Explain me *that*."

"Serves you right," Ted added.

"Don't be stupid," Bob said. "They came to help."

244

"Save your breath," Black cut in. "Get some rest and leave some air."

Jake clicked off his light and sat down at my other side.

I won't wake up, I thought as I closed my eyes. This dark will be the last thing I see. There was a lot of shifting and coughing in the hall. Ro rested her head on my shoulder.

I woke up suddenly, surprised that I had been asleep, and took a slow, deep breath. Cool air flowed into my lungs. Ro was curled up against me. The ventilation, I realized, had also brought heat into the hall. We might freeze long before we stopped breathing.

"You awake?" Jake whispered at my right.

"Have we been asleep long?"

"Six hours by my timer."

"Shouldn't you be with Linda?"

"She wanted to be by herself—don't worry, she's okay."

"Do you think the cop station leads anywhere?"

"You're thinking of punching through the blocked vent," he said.

"It's better than this."

"We might strike pure vacuum. And vacuums abhor people who try to breathe them. Might as well risk opening the front door."

"True," I said, "but if there were people in the room

245

beyond the blocked vent, they probably kept their door to the tunnel closed."

I heard him sit up. "Possible—I should have thought of it. Must be lack of oxygen. So we won't breathe vacuum—but what else will it get us?"

"Bob," I whispered.

"I heard," he said. "Two tunnels lead off from the station. The same one we have out front, and one from the back."

"There should have been another way out of here too," I said.

"We planned to melt through another," Bob said.

"Look," Jake said, "even if we can't go anywhere from the station, we might get some air flowing in here."

"Maybe," Bob replied.

"Hey—shut up!" a male voice whispered loudly from the floor.

"I already know the shaft," I said. "Is there something I can dig with?"

Jake turned on his flashlight, stood up, and moved toward the screen unit, where he bent over and squatted under the console. After a minute of scraping and squeezing noises, he unbolted a meter length of shiny steel. "This should do," he said as he brought it to me.

I took my light and turned it on. It seemed to be working, so I attached its magnetic surface to one end of the rod and gave the assembly to Jake.

"Shine the light at the opening," I said.

I climbed up on his shoulders and pulled myself inside. Then I turned and reached down for the steel.

"I'll come up and stay at the mouth," Jake said as he handed it up. "Yell if you need help."

"Right." I crawled inside, pointing the beam ahead.

Breathing became harder again. I slowed, inhaling evenly. No point in passing out.

Rest, I told myself as I came to the turn, but I didn't stop; every delay would leave me weaker. I was stirring up dust. My eyes filled with tears and I began coughing.

Closing my eyes tightly, I felt my way forward until I touched the grating with my rod. I put it down and took out a handkerchief. Wheezing, I struggled to tie the cloth around my face.

I began to spit, bringing up gobs of dusty mucus, drooling over myself. I thought I was going to throw up, but the heaving stopped as the fabric over my nose and mouth began its filtering action. I was still getting stuffy air, but it was cleaner.

I lay down and rested, breathing slowly until I felt better; then I forced myself up on all fours again.

Removing the light from the rod, I placed the beam to shine on the grating. Slowly, I struck the rocky debris, pushing the rod through the grating to loosen the material on the other side.

There might just as well be a hundred light-years of

stone ahead of me, I thought, and even if I broke through, there might not be any air on the other side.

I jabbed at the rock a hundred times, goaded on by visions of it falling away. People would die if I failed. Rosalie would die.

The light flickered. I reached over and turned it off, angry at its old design; everything on Mercury was obsolete. I knew the small space well enough by now to work in the dark. Might as well save the light, whatever there was left of it.

I picked at the wall of rubble, insisting to myself that I would find myself on the other side if I didn't weaken. My future self was waiting only a few minutes up ahead, alive and out of danger. I needed him, even if he no longer needed me.

As I worked and sweated in the dark, I wished that he would reach across from his side of time and pull me through the rock to safety. . . .

My heart was beating wildly as I chopped at the grating, ready to explode in my chest; and the blackness flowed in around me, imprisoning me as it solidified.

17 THE SQUEEZE

All the air had disappeared into the future.

I lay still in an endless present, unable to breathe, eyes open, listening to the dark, wondering if they were all dead back in the hall.

Something shifted, gritty and stonelike; a trembling passed through me. I strained to hear beyond the pounding of blood in my ears, fearful that the coming quake would crush me.

Then a soft breeze wandered in from the future, slipping into the pocket of the past where I was trapped. I pulled the coolness into my lungs and waited for the fresh air to dry my face. I inhaled deeply, and with a jolt my body resumed its forward motion in time.

I sat up suddenly and groped for my light.

"Joe!" Jake's echo stabbed into my ears.

"I'm okay!" I found the light and turned it on.

"Air's flowing," Jake called.

I turned the light on the grating and saw a small

opening at the top right-hand corner, where the tremor had probably loosened the rockfall.

I seized the rod and began to widen the break. When the breach was larger, I put down the rod and positioned myself to use my feet.

I kicked.

The grate gave a bit on the second try, more on the third.

I gulped a deep breath and whacked it a good one. The grate sailed away into the darkness. I listened to its clattering, unable to believe my luck.

I heard coughing. "Who's there?" I demanded.

"Need help?" Bob answered.

"Come ahead—I've cleared it!"

"Joe?" Rosalie asked from what seemed a great distance.

I cast the light into the tunnel and saw her. Linda and Bob were behind her. "We felt the airflow," Bob said.

"What kind of room is behind us?" I asked.

"The floor of the jail is no lower than in the hall," he answered.

"Go on through," Linda said impatiently.

I turned the light and crawled through the grate opening. Perching on the rubble, I searched the room with my beam. It was a cell block.

"It's the jail, all right," I said, realizing that the barred doors might be locked from the outside. I was squatting on a huge pile of rock that had fallen against the wall, high enough to cover the vent. The ceiling of the chamber was cracked, threatening more falls.

Bob crawled out next to me.

"There's no one here," I said, illuminating the rubble all the way to the bars.

"Might mean they got out. The doors may be open."

I started down, but my foot caught on something. My light revealed a human arm, and for a moment I wondered if by some miracle it had grown out of the rubble. The palm was open, as if to shake hands. I checked the pulse, but the limb was stiff and cold.

"Dead?" Bob asked.

"Yes."

"Hey!" Jake called from the far end of the shaft. "The lights have gone on in the hall!"

Bob poked his head back into the opening. "Try the screen intercom again!"

"Doing it now!"

We waited.

"No luck! There go the lights again!"

I scrambled lower and turned to give Bob some light. He reached me and we picked our way to the bars. "Whose hand would that be?" I asked.

"Probably one of the recent ex-cons."

"You lock them up?"

"Oh, no. He might have been in for being drunk, or something. Many of them use the jail to sleep in. We don't have room and they don't mind."

"You mean they keep to themselves."

"Some do, some don't. If they marry, they live differently, but that doesn't happen too often."

Bob grasped the bars with both hands and pushed. I helped and we managed to slide the door open. He took out his flashlight and played the beam back over the rubble.

"I hope most of them got out," he said. "Come on down!"

Linda and Rosalie crawled out of the vent and made their way down the pile. Neither of them stopped or said anything when they saw the hand.

"Listen," Bob said.

"What?"

"Air—coming in from the other shafts."

I heard a steady whisper.

Linda and Ro reached us and Bob led the way out into the station. We saw no more bodies. The place was deserted, even though the damage seemed light. I wondered how many bodies might be hidden by the rubble in the cell blocks.

"This is the complaint room," Bob said.

Empty chairs faced the judicial bench. The screen was flashing a ghostly light across the wall behind the bench, reminding me of fish swimming in an aquarium.

Bob sat down behind the bench and punched up a call on the terminal.

"Can't get anything," he said finally.

"What now?" Linda asked, sounding strangely composed.

Bob looked up at us, his face pale in the flicker. "Well—we can't risk opening the outer door to the tunnel from here either. We're right next to the hall, but we're getting air in here and it's moving through to the others. We're all safe for the moment. I don't want to do anything to make things worse. We can last a long time with air."

We all sat down in the first row of chairs.

"They'll get to us eventually," Bob said from the bench. "The Heat Mole digger always comes through damaged tunnels and reseals them."

"But when?" Linda asked.

"Could be a few days, but there's a kitchen in here. We can move some of the kids out of the hall—"

"What if it's so bad they can't do anything for us?" Linda insisted. "Shouldn't we face that possibility?"

"Unlikely," Bob replied, shaking his head. Again, he seemed unwilling to admit that it could happen. "If it drags on, the asteroid people will arrive and lend a hand. We can last a long time with food and air. . . ."

"Bob," I said gently, "could they be all dead? How

would we know?" I glanced at Linda. Her dark shape was watching me.

"The Control Center can withstand anything. They'll get us out."

Linda sighed. "People have been dying here."

"I said the Control Center, not the whole place." His voice trembled.

"Hello!"

"That's Jake," I said, standing up.

I rushed back into the cell block. Jake was crouching inside the vent, shining his light down. His beam caught me in the eyes as I reached the bars.

"Will someone tell me what's going on?" he said.

"Start bringing people through. Bob says there's a kitchen."

"Can we fit everyone?" he asked.

"We'll call a halt if it gets crowded."

He stared at me for a moment. I blinked and he was gone.

The first group was coming through when the cell block ceiling caved in again. I heard the sound and started toward the block.

"Don't!" Bob shouted from the console, where he had been working to contact the Control Center.

"They may need help!"

"Should have stayed," Linda muttered.

I listened for tremors, clicked on my light and approached the doorway. Dust was drifting out, a stately motion of particles wandering in my beam.

Coughing, Jake and a few kids staggered out. I flicked my beam across them, looking for signs of injury. Linda and Ro rushed up to them, and we settled them into chairs.

I went through the door and down the short corridor, and saw that all six cells were filled in with rockfall. I couldn't even see where the ceiling had been. I turned and staggered back.

"How many were with you?" I asked Jake.

"Seven or eight more—but some were still in the pipe, so they'll make it back into the hall."

"We're cut off," I said. "The hall is not getting air again."

I looked around in the ghostly light. Ten of us had gotten out—ten out of a couple of hundred.

"Who's here?" I asked.

Bob called out their names: "Helen Wodka, Ted Quist, Jenny Miller, Frank Givenchy, Hank Golden."

"Sergeant Black was right behind me . . ." Helen said.

"Did he come out of the vent?" I asked.

She nodded.

I turned off my flashlight and we sat in silence for a few moments. The flickering screen cast Bob's shadow on the wall behind the bench. He was hunched over, working intently to reach through the intercom lines, and it seemed that he was playing a strange game of some sort.

"Who else came out of the vent?" I asked.

"I was next to last," Helen replied.

"So he's the only one we lost." Not counting those who were already under the rockfall, I thought, and assuming no one was crushed in the pipe.

"Maybe we should try to dig through to the vent," I said.

"With what?" Jake asked. "It would take a week."

"I don't hear the air coming in," Helen said suddenly.

We listened to the silence, hoping that it was just a trick of hearing.

"The inlet's here above the bench," Bob said.

I turned my torch on it. He climbed up and held his hands against the grate. "Nothing—it's blocked."

He jumped down and slumped into his place behind the screen, and I realized that the air system was being cut at more than one point.

"The sensors at Control have to be showing which air lines are gone," Bob insisted. "They must know the fix we're in by now."

If the feedback warning system was still intact; if there was anyone to read the sensors. I had no doubt that someone would get us out. Eventually. Dead or alive. It just didn't seem likely that we'd remedy our local lack of air *twice*. How much luck can you have in one day? Breathing was beginning to seem a luxury.

I had a wild thought.

"Bob—can't we get up to the surface and cross over to the Center? There are only ten of us."

He stared at me from across the room, his face distorted by the cold flickering. The strain of the last hours was beginning to show. He no longer seemed sure of anything. Maybe his parents were dead, he was telling himself; after all, they were flesh and blood, as easily crushed as the people in the cell blocks. They weren't immune—anyone could be dead. It seemed clear to me that Bob knew by now that this situation was different from the ones he had survived in the past. The quake had probably affected a larger area, and there were other things to consider.

"There are hatches to the surface," he said finally, "and we could probably find a few suits, but—"

"You and I'll go for help. They may not know—"

"—but the Sun is up," he said, shaking his head in despair. "Even with a suit it would be like sunbathing in the light of a million thermonuclear bombs."

"Then why have suits at all!" I shouted angrily.

"It's pretty safe at night."

His face darkened and faded away as the screen died, leaving us in total darkness.

"Save the flashlights," Jake said.

257

"Isn't anything good enough?" I asked.

"Sure—the shielded vehicles," Bob replied, "but if there's a solar flare, forget it. Nothing will do. Instant crisp human."

Jake snorted.

"Are there any vehicles nearby?" I asked. Questioning him was like pulling teeth. He seemed dazed.

"Don't know."

"Well, let's go find out!"

"You'd still have to cross some surface to get one."

"What if one were close by?"

"We could make a dash for it, but the radiation dose might still be bad. . . ."

"Tell them the truth," Jake said.

We waited. "I'll be very honest—it's never been this long. Too much seems to have gone wrong this time. Pockets like this may be all that's left."

"So you don't think we're going to make it," Linda said.

"I've lived here all my life. You get a feeling . . ."

I stood up in the darkness. "Feelings, my ass! Where's the hatch, the suits?"

"Could use a suntan myself," Jake said. "Always wondered what it would be like to look that big Sun in the face." I couldn't tell if he was joking.

"Maybe we should just wait," Helen Wodka said.

"If there are hatches, they were meant to be used," I insisted. "Where are the suits?"

258

"I think we can reach one of the utility rooms," Bob said cautiously. "There's a door to your right."

I turned on my flashlight and found it.

"I'll go with you," Bob said.

I walked over and tried the crank. It turned easily.

"Crank it shut after us," Bob instructed.

"What if you don't come back?" Linda asked.

"Then you'll just have to wait for help," Bob replied as I cranked open the door.

Ro came up to me. "Joe—are you sure you want to try this?"

"There's no choice," I whispered. "The air in here or in the hall won't last forever." Bob took my flashlight and shone it into a long, dark corridor. I put my arms around Ro and held her close. "Do you want me to wait here and watch you suffocate?"

We kissed. "I just wanted to know that you feel sure about going," she said.

I turned away quickly and followed Bob. We heard the door cranking shut behind us.

"Here it is," he said as we came to another door.

I turned the crank. The door opened and we stepped inside. Half a dozen suits hung on the racks.

"These are useless against the Sun," he said wearily, "and it's more than two kilometers to the Center. We can't dash that." He had lived here all his life. What could I possibly know?

"Wait a minute," he said suddenly.

"I'm thinking the same thing—we'll have to go up and see."

"I don't know. There may be no way to check except by opening the airlock." He still didn't sound too hopeful.

"If we could get to the Center," I said, "we could come back in a shielded track bus, dock with the airlock, and take everyone out. We could do that, couldn't we?"

"It would be funny if we died out there and help arrived anyway."

"We could be just as dead thinking like that," I said. "How long can they last back in the hall?"

"Let's suit up," he said.

We held the light for each other, and checked each suit as we put it on. Our helmet lights went on when we closed our face plates.

"These are ancient," Bob said over the suit com. "Not much use for them." He pointed upward. "Let's go."

My helmet beam shot up into a rock chimney. A ladder rose for at least thirty meters and disappeared into the dark.

We climbed, listening to each other's breathing. The suits seemed to be working well, despite their age.

"Stop," Bob said after a long while. "Here's the inner lock crank." I heard him struggling above me. "Okay, it's open." His feet disappeared into the opening. Lights came on.

I climbed up after him. "The lights work in here," I said.

"Independent source. Solar."

"What now?"

"You stay here." He started to crank the door to the outer chamber. Suddenly the door slid open. "Must have triggered an automatic."

I followed him inside, ignoring his instructions. The inner door closed behind us.

He pointed. "Look—we'll be able to see!"

There was a small round viewport in the outer door. We could check the Sun's position without having to open the lock.

18 CROSSING

I stood behind Bob as he peered through the thick viewport.

"Can you see anything?"

He gave the port a wipe with his gloved hand. I heard crackling, then his voice in my ear. "We're in the shadow of those cliffs to the left. I think we can walk to the Center."

"You don't sound too sure."

From what I knew, Mercury was crisscrossed with scarps—huge, curving cliffs up to four kilometers high. They were formed when Mercury's crust was cooling and shrinking and massive blocks were being thrust upward along fault lines. One particular cliff, Discovery Rupes, was 500 kilometers long.

"The Sun is low this time of day," Bob continued, "but I can't tell how close it may be to the top of the scarp. It isn't noon yet. We'll have to hurry, in case the Sun clears the top and zaps us."

"Is that all?" A few kilometers in low gravity was not going to be difficult, but I was thinking only of myself.

"I don't know if the surface lock to the Center is in shadow or not. I've never come this way."

"So we may have to sprint a few yards."

The crackling filled my ears. "We can't do that, Joe. Get that through your head. Not in this suit or any other. By the way, have you ever walked around in a suit?"

"No."

"Move carefully—don't let it get damaged."

"Do we have enough air?"

"They're rebreathers," he said. "Packs can recycle in-definitely."

"Okay—let's go."

He tapped the door control with his fist. The door slid open and we stepped out slowly onto the coppery surface.

I looked up, grateful to see the stars. Somewhere out there, away from the Sun, was Venus, orbiting only 50 million kilometers away; and Earth, 91 million kilometers distant. At my right, the wall of cliffs hid the fiery Sun, which was waiting, it seemed, to rise up and burn us as soon as we started across the shadowland, because it knew that we were out here, and that only chance had given us the protection we needed.

To my left was a sea of light. There the shadows came to a sharp end. Slowly, as the Sun climbed, that sea would creep toward the cliffs, dissolving the shadowland; we would be forced against the base of the scarp if we stayed out long enough. At noon there would be almost no place to hide; the solar eye would cook us with its fusion gaze. . . .

"I think the locks to the Control Center are there," Bob said, pointing into the blackness. "If we keep close to the scarp at our right, we'll be protected all the way."

Noon was still weeks away, I told myself. There was no way the Sun could get us, but Bob sounded as if there were other things to fear.

"So what else can get us?" I asked.

"Micrometeorites. They pelt the surface. No atmosphere to burn them up. Go through you like a bullet, if you're hit. Unlikely, but the idea always gives me the creeps."

"We won't be out long enough," I said. "Let's get going."

"Just a moment—I want to try something. Control, please reply, this is Bob Svoboda. . . ."

Of course, the suit radios.

Bob repeated his call a few times, but the only reply was the universe making popcorn.

"Why don't they answer?" I asked.

"It could be a number of things. Quake might have damaged surface antennas. No one's expecting a call from the surface, so there may be nobody listening, nothing more." I knew that he thought it could be something more, but he was determined not to start supposing. "Come on."

I followed, avoiding loose rocks, stepping only where the coppery way seemed firm. It was an easy stroll, despite the bulky suit; but my muscles were used to a higher gravity, so I didn't notice the suit's weight as much as Bob did. I began to stride, then took a small leap forward.

Bob stopped and fixed me with the mirrored eye of his faceplate. My ears crackled. "Don't, Joe—you can still break a limb or tear your suit."

"Sorry."

I thought of Ro as we passed deeper into the shadow of the high cliffs. What would there be for us after we finished working here? More school—and then what? My heart seemed to hesitate between beats as I realized that I might never see Ro again. She was probably thinking the same thing. I faced the possibility that one of us might die.

I glanced up at the scarp. It was hard to feel how tall the cliffs were; they seemed unreal. All of Mercury had been molten once, cooling from the outside in, buckling the outer crust as it formed, forcing sections to pile up on each other while swarms of meteors, even asteroids, bombarded the planet. The scarps were what geologists call thrust faults, where one side of a crack has been raised and the other lowered. On Merk they cut through mountain ranges, craters, and valleys. The Sun's energy had sculpted this world, and left it half finished. The interior was still molten with heavy metals—the ultimate prize, which humankind would claim as we reached deeper into the planet.

We had been marching for about fifteen minutes, pulling our legs up and down like robots, when I felt a gentle trembling in my feet.

Turning to look back, I saw a crack following us, like a beast tracking prey; its speed was deceptive.

"Bob!" I jumped aside and turned around in time to see it shoot toward him like a crooked snake.

I took giant steps and tackled him. My weight threw him clear, but my feet went into the crack as it passed us. It would have been a sorry tackle on Earth, I thought as I reached out and caught the edge.

I hung there.

Bob was about five meters away, down but moving. I pulled myself up, grateful that I was from Earth. Growing up there had all been for this—so I could come here and tackle Bob. Funny what goes through your head in moments of danger.

I got up and walked over to him. He was sitting up, holding his left sleeve. "A small tear," he said, "but I've got a good grip on it."

"Are you hurt?" I asked, realizing that I was responsible—but there had been no choice.

"Fine—but I've got to keep this closed. One day we'll have new equipment."

I reached down and pulled him to his feet.

"Sneaky crack," he said.

"Sure was."

It was still running ahead of us, parallel to the scarp.

"Can you hold that?"

"Sure—let's go."

He tried to lead the way again, but I was at his side.

"It can't be far now," he said.

I peered into the inky shadows ahead. "What's it look like?"

"Silver dome—three meters high."

"Don't see a thing yet."

"It's got to be there!"

I felt his confidence draining away.

"I could have sworn this was the right way, Joe."

"Don't worry—if it's to our right, we can still step over the crack. Hope it doesn't widen."

His breathing seemed more labored over the suit com. "Follow the crack."

"How do you feel?"

"I'm okay!" he insisted.

We marched in silence.

"Look at the pedometer in your helmet," he said. "We've come half a kilometer."

I noticed the ghostly row of dials. When I looked out again, Bob was four meters ahead. I caught up.

"Not much you could do if my suit went," he said.

"Try calling again," I said.

"We'll make it, Joe."

"Bob, play it safe—right now."

"They've got enough to worry about."

"Try."

"We'll get there. Don't you see? Ripping a suit is . . . well, basically a dumb thing."

"But I did it—not you." I saw Kik falling. One gone, one saved. It couldn't count for much with Linda. "We Earthies are pretty clumsy guys. One of your folks would have known better."

"Thanks, Joe." I knew Bob still had his pride; I could hear it in his voice. But he might still try to take the blame for ripping his suit, the kind of mistake only a kid would make. I had to make sure I spoke first and saved him the embarrassment.

I kept looking at his sleeve. His whole hand was closed on the rip. What was a human hand doing on Mercury? I asked myself as we marched. It had grown up in sun-filled forests and on grassy plains, gathering skills for an awakening brain. Too many hands and minds from Earth had died on hostile Mercury. I would get Bob to safety, and I would help build a new world for him to live and work in.

The shadows shaped themselves into faceless figures, closing in to whisper strange thoughts into my head. I was sweating heavily in the suit.

Bob stopped. "We've gone past—can't be this far. Must be on the other side of the crack, back some."

The ground trembled, widening the crack.

"We've got to jump across!" Bob shouted as the other side drifted away from us.

"You can't holding that sleeve."

The trembling stopped.

"It's two meters at least," I said, knowing what I would have to do. "Come here." I stepped toward him and lifted him in my arms, knowing that he had to hold his sleeve and couldn't resist. "I won't leave you out here." He had to arrive with me, as much on his own as possible; it would humiliate him to be left out here while I went for help.

"I feel stupid, Joe."

"Better than being dead," I said, taking a few steps back. "Hold that rip tight."

I went forward and jumped.

We sailed across the crack in a shallow arc, but the slowness made me afraid that we wouldn't make it.

We landed with a meter to spare. I dared to breathe again. My body shook a little.

"You can put me down now."

I set him on his feet. He was silent, clutching his sleeve. "Joe—you won't tell anyone about this. Please."

"Sure—forget it."

"I'll always remember."

"Glad to help. We're all supermen on Earth, so it's no

big deal. Try the radio again. It might be easier if we're closer."

"Svoboda calling Central—please answer."

We listened to the crackling.

"Good thing I can transmit by pressing down with my chin," he said.

"Bob! Where are you?" Robert Svoboda demanded suddenly, his voice clear against the background hiss.

"We came out by the surface lock over the police station," Bob said.

"Get off the surface!"

"Don't worry, Dad—Joe and I are in a safe shadow."

"You've got the greenhorn out there?"

I felt foolish.

"Dad—listen to me! We've got to run a bus over and evacuate the hall. Some people have died. Air's running out. We need digging tools. What's delayed you?"

My ears filled with hiss and crackle.

"What? We don't show any air cutoff on our big board."

"Forget the board! Is the tunnel cutter working?"

"No," his father said, after a moment. "Spare parts problems—they're fixing it."

Bob cursed. "Dad—you've got to get a digging crew into a vehicle, bring it over to the cop station, cut through to the hall and start bringing people out. Police station air won't last forever either!"

"That bad—" Robert Svoboda said softly, defeat in his voice.

"Don't blame him for trying," Eleanor cut in. "We could have all been dead here, for all he knew."

"Son—you took such a risk," Svoboda added.

"Dad—how bad is it elsewhere?"

"Pretty bad, I guess. From what you've said, we can't rely on our sensor board. It's all too old—the whole system is coming apart. . . ."

"Where are you?" Eleanor asked.

"Just near the dome—we think."

"Joe?"

"I'm here . . . Eleanor."

"We're coming in, Dad," Bob said. "Should be a few minutes."

"The asteroid is here," Svoboda announced, "for what it's worth. It's a giant potato on our screens, baking in the Sun. West, thirty degrees high."

We turned and looked above the sea of sunlight. A bright star was rising in its orbit, bringing hope to the miners of Mercury, and I prayed that there would be no more disasters before the habitat was livable.

"We see it!" Bob shouted, his voice catching with emotion.

"Get going," Robert Svoboda said. "I want you two safe as soon as possible."

We broke contact and started back along the widened crack. As I looked at the landscape of white light to our right, I realized how small was our area of safety.

We stopped suddenly. A great shaft of sunlight had

broken through the scarp some kilometers ahead, burning through the shadow zone to rejoin the Sun-blasted
plain.

"There must be a pass up there," Bob said, "and the
Sun moved into position to shine through."

I looked around, suddenly afraid of hidden breaks in
the cliffs. The idea of playing peekaboo with a nearby
fusion furnace did not appeal to me. Old Sol, grand
light of all Sunspace, might still get us. He didn't
like the creatures he had cooked up out of the pri-
mordial slime to get too close to him. I saw my body
sprouting cancerous cauliflowers as it stood in a giant
sunbeam. . . .

"There's . . . dome!" Bob shouted, losing a word in
the static.

My eyes found the small hemisphere huddling in the
shadows, daring to reflect a bit of starlight.

We moved toward it.

"Watch it," I said. The cracks were all pointing to the
dome as if to a target.

"They're small. As long as we can reach one of the
locks."

We were about fifty feet away when the ground shook
again. The cracks opened and I rolled into one.

I tensed, but it took forever to hit.

Finally I felt scraping and pressure from two sides.
My wrist snapped and pain jolted into my elbow and

shoulder. I was caught between the narrowing walls of the fissure.

"Joe!"

"Get inside," I ordered as calmly as I could, "and send someone without a damn hole in their suit."

"Keep talking!"

"Get going!"

"Try not to move."

"Are you still here?"

Merk had me in its teeth. It had been waiting for me since the time when the planets formed. At the slightest tremor, its angry jaws would crush me; or the crack would yawn and I would be swallowed.

"Can you breathe?"

"Yes—get moving," I managed to say. "Now it's your turn."

The universe hissed at me. Mercury, the Sun's henchman, would kill me, or at least maim me, because the earthies had not cared enough to protect their own against him.

I drew a deep breath; it tasted wrong.

"Bob?"

There was no answer on the suit com. I tried to press my chin down inside the helmet, to open the radio channel to the Control Center, but I couldn't move my head.

"Bob," I whispered, "there's something wrong with my air."

The universe shoved itself into my head—a million gears grinding away, rending and tearing by fits and stops, as if trying to shape abusive sentences. Alien stars sang deep inside the chaos in my head. Solid black cement crept in around me, tucking in close, filling my lungs. I stopped breathing, grateful that I would no longer have to make the effort.

19 LOOKING BACK

The sun reached out with fiery knives and cut away my arm and leg. . . .

I swam through a sea of molten metal, under a giant red Sun, struggling to reach the icy coolness of the rock before the liquid metal burned through to my bones. . . .

Rosalie waited for me on the rock. I loved her, desired and needed her more than ever—but my hands were skeletons when I pulled myself up on the soothing shore. . . .

As the painkillers wore off, my dislocated shoulder and broken wrist, together with a touch of oxygen starvation, taught me a lot of respect for old Merk. I was so glad to be alive that I wished I might have broken the other wrist, just so as not to push my luck.

I lay there for more than a month, wondering if the planet was really done with me; a new quake might kill me as I slept. Bob and Rosalie calmed me down in the evenings, but I still had trouble accepting sleep.

When I was finally able to doze regularly, my dreams were filled with guilt and anxiety about the work that was starting without me. If I wasn't going to be part of the work, then everything that had happened to me would be meaningless. I was fixated on this, even though there was no chance of the habitat being finished before I got there.

Sometimes I dreamed that I was dying by pieces— first my legs, then my arms and torso, leaving only my head, which was not enough to go home with; they would probably just throw it away.

"Bob told us how you helped save his life," Robert Svoboda said, as he and his wife sat by my bed one day.

"He still had to hold his suit together."

Eleanor touched my hand. "He felt differently about telling us after you were both inside."

I looked up at the ceiling and felt very unheroic. "We might both have died."

"Couldn't expect you not to try something," Robert said. "I'm glad you did, as it turned out. The judgments you two made about the situation were right. Bob learned a few things. Eleanor and I had always shielded him a bit from things."

"I want to get to my real job as soon as possible."

Eleanor's look of gratitude was making me nervous. It surprised me that Bob had decided to tell the whole story. How would it go over with his friends? Maybe it would draw us all together.

Bill Turnbull, my orientation advisor from the university, surprised me with a visit one Friday afternoon.

"I joined up with the second wave," he said. "Brought you some letters from home."

"Thanks—how's the work going?"

"Can't go on without you," he said cheerfully, putting the sealed fax-letter copies on my table. "Half the workers are on the asteroid, building temporary quarters on the inner surface. The engineers took all the livable space in the construction sphere." He smiled. "Don't lie around here too long."

I stared at the letters after he left, afraid to open them; if you don't feed old problems, they fade away.

I picked up one and tore it open:

25 May 2057, Bernal Hall, BERNAL ONE

Dear Joe,

        I don't know if you want to
    hear from me or not out there
    where you're pioneering. I heard
    your name on the news, among
    those who were injured, so I
    decided you should hear from me.

        I guess you were always a
    practical sort, looking for a
    place to shine. I know I said not
    much could be done about the
    Mercury problem, and I'm still
    skeptical, but I didn't expect

you to go and make yourself part
of the solution, such as it is—
hats off!

I still hope that you'll come
back to school sooner or later.
You might make a good *experimental* physicist, with your
practical turn of mind. You
always seemed to need people
around to do things with. Me, I
still think life is for the private struggle to understand the
universe, the way Einstein or
Hawking struggled to climb the
mountain of knowledge in their
minds—just to see if they could
see nature whole.

Morey still sounded a million years old, but I would
have been disappointed if he had changed.

Maybe I have to shut out
everything else, just to be able
to do what I want? Sometimes I
can't bear to think that there
are other roads in life, or that
I might want to take them and
forget the slow climb toward the
wall of mystery that is physics.
If there is anything that you
want very much, then you *must*
know what I mean.

There's no rush, you know. The biologists say people our age may make it to 200, if not more. I think you'll feel the pull of study again when you're older. Some people appreciate knowing things more when life gets chancy.

Now that I'm well into the big math and talking smoothly to the artificial brain cores, I find that I'm developing all sorts of neat suspicions about the universe—as if it were some sort of stage scenery. Tell you more in the next letter.

So—even though I think striving for achievement is everything, accomplishments may vary, even go unseen. I didn't see what you wanted, but now that I feel I'm getting closer to what I want, and don't feel so desperate about moving along, I see what I might be missing along the way. You pay for everything somewhere. If I don't concentrate stubbornly, I won't get what I want. Only luck, that sudden, unearned input of energy from somewhere else, enables us to sometimes come out ahead.

        I guess I think most people are
    pretty hopeless—they live and
    don't do much that I can see,
    except to secure their lives and
    the lives of their children.
    Maybe most humanity isn't ready
    for much more yet.

        Write when you can, or leave
    messages. David, Marco, and
    Narita say hello.

                    Your friend, Morey

Good old Morey, I thought as I put the letter on my
night table. For once he made me feel that it didn't have
to be an either/or choice. Distant moments of achievement were worth working for, if you could see that far.
I hadn't been able to do it on Bernal, but his letter made
me feel good—not so threatened about making another
choice. Scratch that problem. I would have called him
immediately, but the delays between answers would have
been frustrating, even if Merk had been in position to
avoid static interference from the Sun.

    I glanced uneasily at the envelopes from my parents;
it seemed that their words were waiting to drag me back
into my childhood. I scooped up the letters and opened
one.

    It was from Dad:

23 May 2057, NEW YORK CITY

Dear Joe,

   We heard that you were
injured, but the Svobodas
assured us that it was not
serious enough for us to come
out, but if you want us there
we'll take the next ship out. I'm
told that there are quite a few
going back and forth these days,
twice a month, in fact. I hear
it's pretty rugged there.

   Write or leave a message when
you get this. Call if you want
and solar conditions permit.
I'll sit through the delays.

                              Love, Dad

P.S. You might like to hear that
Marisa has gone right into
commercial art. Her loop
sequences, mostly landscapes,
are replacing quite a few
picture windows in the large
cities.

   I looked at the "We heard" part of the letter. Of
course, they weren't together. Old habits die hard. Was

he trying to lure me back home with news of Marisa?
Probably not; he just thought I'd be interested. I was—
mildly.

I opened the last letter.

16 May 2057, BRASILIA

Dearest Joe,

I was worried sick about your
being hurt. I passed the news
that it was nothing serious to
your father and grandparents,
but I won't really feel right
until you write or call with
details. Please don't keep me in
suspense!

I've been studying and reading
a lot. Jim and I live out here on
his ranch. He's an Australian,
but he spent a lot of time on
Luna. He's very impressed with
your decision to work on Mercury. Says he understands
you, and he's been explaining to
me.

I sometimes think that if I
were your age I would have done
the same thing. Your father and I

are on amiable terms, so please
don't worry about that, my son.

Write soon.

Love, Mom

Scratch another problem.
I was completely on my own, and it felt good.

20 THE HABITAT

By the time I got up to the asteroid in mid-July, the rocky inner surface of the hollow was dotted with the lights of work camps, creating an atmosphere of underground gloom within the ten-kilometer-long space. A gentle spin had been put on the big potato, a tenth-g to start, to make it easier to move around. Teams of specialists were hard at work, even as the rest of the workers and equipment continued to arrive.

Bob and I came in through the big locks at one end of the hollow world. As we passed inside and looked out across the open space, I thought of all the work that still had to be done. It was hard to imagine that these hundreds of square kilometers of rock and mud would ever begin to look like the out of doors I had come to know on Bernal.

But it would; I knew it would—as surely as Bernal's inner surface had been changed from a curving plane of metal. When the rock crunchers finished their work, carefully balanced humus would be mixed in to create a layer of rich soil over the bedrock; ground water would run into the lakes and streams cut for it; nitrogen-fixing trees would be put in, along with plants and shrubs that did not need fertilizer, along with a select number of insects, snails, and small animals; finally, human beings would invade the landscape and make it their own.

It sounds easy when you leave out all the detailed steps, but it's hard to make an ecology work; everything is related to everything else and you can get unexpected results if you don't do the measurements right. Strip mining during the last century on Earth had taught us the difficulties of restoring damaged ecosystems, but imagine building one from scratch.

Fortunately, our specialists had done it all before, mistakes and all.

"This seems like work for a god," I said, surveying the barrenness, "not for human beings. Can't even imagine starting on the towns. A year or two won't be enough."

"Just do the land," Bob replied, "and leave the houses to us. It'll be much easier than what we had to build on Mercury."

I sniffed. "Air isn't very tasty." It had been put in out in the Asteroids, using oxygen cracked from an ice asteroid. Industrial recyclers were cleaning up the CO_2, but the strain on the machines was becoming more noticeable as more workers arrived.

"Better than suits," Bob said. "We'll last until the trees and plants take over."

"I suppose."

"Mom always wanted an open-air patio and garden."

"She'll have it all."

"Is it time?" I asked.

"Any moment now," he said.

We gazed across the hollow, waiting. There was a distant sound from the other end, like soft thunder or something opening. I strained to see by the starlight of the work camps.

Slowly, the far end of the asteroid began to glow a dull red, brightening suddenly as the optical systems flooded the hollow with the tamed yellow-white glare of the Sun. The feeling of being deep underground was gone. A desert of rock and varicolored sands presented us with its first sunrise.

Seeing the lights go on in this drafty, dusty hollow moved me deeply, lighting me up inside, making me feel at last that I was going to be myself, and that I had found my way to what I needed.

And I realized that the Sunspace Settlements were everything that the New World had tried to be—a place where humankind could begin the world all over again, free of the Old World's conflicts. America had failed, as Earth had failed, until the sky had been opened, making available the riches of Sunspace, giving humanity its first chance at a genuine high-energy, high-technology society, in which scarcity would no longer be the measure of economic value; *that* evil, at least, would die.

The problem of Mercury was a shameful throwback to the twentieth century, maybe even to the nineteenth, but it would soon be a thing of the past. Thirty people had died in the last quake; over a hundred had been injured. Bernie had been crushed in our room. His ashes were here now, mixed with the soil materials of the habitat. There was nothing special about that; most organic materials were recycled in some way, but I thought it was fitting anyway. For me he would always be here, alive in the land we were about to shape, as active in my mind as he was in the mind of Bernal.

"Good morning," I said finally.

"It's really late afternoon," Bob replied with a straight face. "We'll have to adjust that on the clocks."

We laughed, and a great sense of relief came over me. I had brooded over Bernie's death for some weeks, remembering that last moment in the tunnel when we had said good night so casually. It was so wrong for him to be killed right after he had regained his health. I remembered our first meeting, when he had emerged from Bernal's depths, and I knew what he would say about his death. What did we expect? That we could come here to right a great wrong and expect to be untouched by it? I could almost hear the sound of his piping voice, and I knew that he was right.

But did it have to be you, Bernie?

* * *

I learned to run one of the crunchers, mind-linking with the machine for six hours a day. We had regular days now, with vitamin-D sunlight, which helped our biorhythms. I bit into the asteroid and ripped out huge chunks of rock, swallowing and digesting each mouthful. A fine powder spilled out the back and was mixed with organics. Dark squares of fertile land were laid over the bedrock desert, all around the curve of the world.

I also linked with the beam diggers, helping to cut the groove for the equatorial river. The lake basin was by far the prettiest piece of work we did in the first six months.

During the Christmas holidays, the engineers set up large screens throughout the hollow and fed us transmissions from Earth while we worked; it was the only way of doing something festive for five thousand people. Relatives appeared and recited sappy wishes in a dozen languages. I almost didn't recognize Mom when she came on: confident, beautiful, and adventurous-looking in her plain work clothes; an entirely new person, which she was, in a sense. Ro saw my father, but I was not at the right screen at that moment. I did get a message from him, telling me how much more gift credit had been added to my account.

The miners had a pretty homey Christmas down on bouncy old Merk, but there was no way they could have invited five thousand guests. Ro and I had to turn down the invitation from the Svobodas; we didn't want to seem like privileged characters, even if there had been enough shuttles in good working order. Besides, I was a bit wary of putting myself in Merk's clutches again.

Bob came up with a basket of goodies, and spent some time with us in our tent. The ship from Earth arrived with a better class of food that week, so we did pretty well. Still, I was glad when the holidays were over. It was nice the way Earth kept us company via the screen-relay casts, but the giant figures were at times irritating.

At the start of 2058, Rosalie and I were living in make-shift barracks; depending on where the day's work took us, that's where we would find a bunk. It was a big improvement over tents. Sometimes I wouldn't see her for weeks at a time. She was part of the group bringing up waste materials from Mercury. I worried about her a lot.

As the crunchers finished munching, large waste tanks went up in each sector, and slowly the treated organics were turned into the soil. The amalgam smelled a bit, but after a time it began to give off the odor of rich, black earth. I was surprised at how much waste human beings could produce.

Think of a huge shallow pot made of rock and fill it with soil; that's what the inside of the asteroid was, ba-sically. There was always the chance that the organic fill would die or dry out before we put in the growing things;

a few sectors failed once or twice, which depressed many of us, but the bio-ecologs just shrugged and started again. When you listened to them, they sounded like a bunch of gardeners.

We laid the land deep, more than five meters in some places; you could dig down into the rock if you needed deeper basements. It was still a few hundred meters to the outer surface of the big potato, more than enough shielding from solar radiation—more, in fact, than you get from Earth's atmosphere. One of the advantages in building inside a hollow asteroid is that you don't have to provide sunstorm shelters for your workers. Building a habitat on the Bernal or O'Neill cylinder model requires a large number of solar radiation shelters until the main shielding is in place. Shelters are small and cramped, limiting the size of the work force; the asteroid provides immediate safety for a large number of workers, as well as serving as a base for future construction projects nearby, which can then follow any desired model.

There were some disagreements about landscaping. The miners had their ideas and we had ours; but since we were doing so much of the work, many of our planners felt we should decide. The ecologs insisted that they knew best what would work in the long run. They didn't care what else the miners did inside the hollow, as long as they left the biocomponents alone; the mother-nature crew got its own way in the end. Mostly.

They started losing interest by the time the job was half done and most of the serious problems were under control; new challenges were waiting—like the Ceres project, which was just beginning out in the Asteroids.

The quick-grow trees, plants, and bushes, insect eggs, snails, fish, and small animals began to arrive long before we were actually ready for them, so we piled them in large dumps on the empty land—crates and cages, big pots, bags of special food and spot fertilizers, and mysterious sealed containers with printed notices warning you to play the enclosed instructions. At first we couldn't get enough stuff shipped from Earth, and we had to wait around for things we needed; later we couldn't stop the flow. I was astonished at how much human beings could produce when they wanted to. Eventually we used up everything, and it turned out to be just enough; someone had done a neat job of planning.

The hills of the hollow sloped gently. Three shallow valleys hugged the river, whose banks were steep to allow for gradual wear; the lake was deep and cool, just right for a nearby vineyard or two. The ecologs got the air movements right—a gentle breeze between periods of stillness. The oppressive Sun of Mercury's lifeless landscape was merely warm here, its intensity trapped within an image of itself, varying to drive the weather and nourish the greenery and people, dimming into moonlight at night; it was a dutiful Sun.

There were no extreme seasons. The thermometer might fall to ten degrees centigrade, but only because the population wanted it. Well, almost everyone wanted it that way when the meeting to decide such matters had been called.

As we completed the heavy work, half the population of Mercury was already building houses, while the other half continued hurling tribute at Earth; a surplus of metal slugs had been achieved because of the high morale, and production did not suffer. Earth was getting more consideration than it deserved. Luckily, the next year and a half saw only a few minor quakes.

House building went quickly, but the codes required that each dwelling or town unit fit into the habitat's water, electrical, and communications system, as well as into the carrying capacity of the ecological measurements; this meant a lot of inspection and correction work.

The habitat's spin was increased to simulate fifty percent of Earth's gravity, and the orbit was made synchronous, high over the mining territories, so that the Sun's energy could be pumped constantly. Power could now be beamed down to Mercury's surface during the night by the habitat's outrider beam units.

About half the workers were rotated in the first two years; as the load lightened, specialists left for new jobs in other parts of Sunspace. Ro and I had no plans. Our credit in the bank was growing, so we decided to stay as long as we were needed. We were free to go, but we felt reluctant to do so.

Almost everyone I had known from school had gone home by 2060—to another job, or back to school. Rosalie, Linda, Jake, and I were the only ones left. About ten percent of the original work force were staying on as trial settlers.

There was a new spirit among the miners, who could now be sure that their families were safe while the shifts went down to Merk. All dangers could not be banished; quakes and accidents could not be controlled completely, but at least it was possible to get away from danger on a regular basis.

One day, when it seemed that there was nothing to do, Ro and I accepted an invitation to the new Svoboda house just outside the town in Valley One. Rosalie and I were living in the new hotel, where we were on call for small jobs. There were still some kinks in the water and electrical systems. I couldn't do much in recycling, for example, but Bernie had trained me well in electricity, wet and dry plumbing, ceramic carpentry, and in checking a variety of safety and sensing devices. That was my real specialty—troubleshooting safety sensors, knowing when they were giving reasonable feedback to the brain cores. I earned a certificate in this line of work. The closer we got to being done, the more it seemed that there were still a million things left to do. It was hard to say at what point the work ended and became maintenance.

As Ro and I approached the two-floor ceramic module house—it was shaped to suggest a small Swiss castle of the nineteenth century—I realized how much the people were becoming an actual part of our handiwork. The land was green, in part, because of organic waste recycling, and the chain of interdependence reached all the way back to Earth, into human history, and the evolution of life. Human imagination, shaking itself free of past restraints, had created space habitats. Human needs had built the mining community on Mercury. And now we had transplanted and enriched the energy systems of that community, made its use of the Sun and Mercury more humane. Formed when the solar system had been young, this asteroid was no longer a lump of rock and minerals; it had been infected with life, with mind.

At the top of the hill, a few yards from the house, Ro and I turned and saw spring blossoms floating in the river. Clouds drifted in the bright central space. The sun stood guard at the far end of the world. Overhead, the lake was a sparkling mirror. The stars were beneath our feet, just beyond the rocky crust. It was the newness of this world that impressed me daily. Earth's natural history did not apply here, yet a bit of old Earth was beginning anew.

"Well, hello!" Eleanor said behind us. We turned and saw her standing on her elaborate porch. "The rest are here, you're very late."

I looked at her shyly.

"I know, I know," she said smiling.

Ro looked a bit embarrassed. I took her hand and we followed Eleanor inside, passing into the dining area just off the large living room.

Robert Svoboda sat at the head of the rectangular table. Bob was next to him. Linda and Jake sat at Robert's left. Eleanor seated us at Bob's left, then sat down next to me.

We all smiled. I looked at the handsomely set ceramic table, wondering at how much we had actually changed.

I didn't say much at dinner, but as I listened to Robert, I came to understand something more about the people of Mercury, and about what was happening in this sector of Sunspace.

"We won't be miners forever," he said, "but we've given humankind a better hold on this close-in space around the communal furnace. One day the resources of Mercury may run out, or become unnecessary. Materials synthesis from simpler raw materials is not far off, but when that happens we'll still have world habitats here, an economy, our own way of life. That's what will be important. Human beings are spreading throughout Sunspace. They'll be living in a thousand ways, changing

physically, readying themselves for the stars. This di-
versity will help us if we run into an alien species.We'll
need poets and storytellers to depict these different ways,
just to keep Sunspacer humanity together—in its imaginative self-image, if in no other way." He was looking
at me, as if he expected me to do all these things. It was
right that the town in Valley One was going to be named
after him.

"What will you and Ro do when you're finished?"
Eleanor asked.

"Probably go back to school," I said. "We have more
than enough to take care of ourselves for a few years."

"Maybe we'll go out to the Ceres Project," Ro added.
"I'd like to see an asteroid eight hundred kilometers
across."

I still wasn't certain about anything, but I wasn't worrying about it as much.

Later, I left Ro at the hotel and climbed into the grassy
hills above the town. I felt a bit amused at myself. What
had I proven? I still couldn't see beyond one problem
following another, orbiting the biggest one, myself—the
one I would always have with me. You push back at the
universe and come out ahead. Sometimes. Problems would
never stop coming at me, and I would have to do something about each and every one. They want you to solve
them, and there is nothing else. I wondered if it was
different for Morey. Maybe he had escaped all this, by

giving himself to so much ambitious understanding. It was a way out of himself, and I still admired him for it; but I had to find my own way out of my own maze.

I lay down in the grass and flowers, and gazed up into the hollow. Sunlight was a watercolor yellow-white at this late hour, and would stay that way until morning. I closed my eyes and breathed the cool, sweet air. I wondered about my parents. There had been only a half dozen letters in the last year, but that didn't bother me; they were long letters, even if they didn't settle old problems. . . .

I opened my eyes and saw Bernie standing over me.

"Bernie," I whispered, "you're alive. . . .

"They stopped looking for me, but I dug myself out," he said, smiling, looking the same as when he had come out of the hatch on Bernal.

But then my eyes opened again and I was alone, missing him.

I recalled the faces around the table, remembering the way Robert Svoboda had looked at me. If I left them, it seemed that I would lose myself again. Why is it that your sense of self is so often bound up with people you knew well or grew up with? Does the ego put a headlock on uncertainty by making everything part of itself?

Suddenly I felt that I didn't want to be anything for long. You're never really one thing anyway—except in those moments when you freeze up. Some people do it early and stay that way, unable to change. My messy face of oatmeal was nothing to fear; I was determined to grow as long as the mush held out, as long as I didn't give up. Whole cultures on Earth had died rather than change, believing that Earth was all there could be; they had grabbed bits of it and locked them away behind borders. They didn't know that the stars are suns that burn almost forever, that the universe is rich in all that we will ever need, and we can reach out if we're rich enough inside to see, to think, to imagine—more than anything to *imagine* what can be, to keep it in a store of imaginings and pass it on to our future.

Few people my age in human history had seen what I had seen—but in my time I am not very special in that. Alexander had conquered what he could see of the world at my age—and had complained that there were no others. If he could have left Earth, he would have been humbled by the planet's smallness and the true size of the cosmos; but in his time only cruelty and death could humble the rulers of Earth.

Out here there was no one to steal the land from, as the settlers had from the Indians of the Americas. Space and energy around suns were abundant, but you had to buy these resources with work and caring.

Robert Svoboda cared. Like Bernie, he loved the place where he lived because he had helped create it, becoming part of it, even though he had been born elsewhere; it was as if Mercury had been waiting for him. The miners had taken the Sun's strength into their minds and bodies, and one day that energy would flow out across sunspace not only as resources and physical power, but as art, music, and science. All the conditions for a human society were here, the makings of a culture.

I had been wrong to feel sorry for those trapped here by a lifetime of low gravity. This sector of space was their home, not Earth, however hard living here had been on their parents. I exercised, so I could go back, but they didn't care, even though the habitat's gravity increase would make it easier for their children to travel elsewhere. More habitats would be built, and for future generations of Mercurians the big Sun's light would sing eternal and be part of what they meant by home, until that faraway day when their habitats might choose to become mobile and head out to the stars.

Much of the prejudice against Sunspacers, I learned, had come from the deeply rooted notion that expansion into space meant the settling of other Earthlike planets, not building new worlds from scratch in free space or terraforming hostile planets like Venus and Mars. Free space habitats, I came to believe, were the way to go; you might be stealing nursery environments from un-born intelligences if you settled Earthlike planets, even if a particular world might seem deserted when you arrived. Your coming might actually abort a whole line of evolution.

I got up and looked at the night Sun. Something in

me needed to look out at the stars, so I walked back into town and borrowed one of the bikes from in front of the hotel.

I pedaled off, away from the Sun, toward the rocky, opposite end of the world, wondering if everyone has a special home somewhere, other than the place he grew up in. I thought of my room in New York. Someone else lived there now.

Home may be where you were born, or it may be elsewhere, even in more than one place; it may be no-where, for some people. I was still looking around. Maybe it would be back on Earth, out in the Asteroids, or even here.

The road branched and climbed before me. I pumped up the left turn toward the lock tunnel. Above me loomed the unfinished, rocky narrows of the world. I cycled to the large metal door and dismounted. Laying down the bike, I turned and gazed across the length of the hollow.

The night Sun stood guard over the sleeping valleys. Lake and river were pale silver, hills blue-green in the soft light. There was a chill in the air, and I noticed something. There was very little sense here of a mys-terious nature which had been here before we appeared. Like Bernal, this world was younger than humanity; only the Sun and rock were ancient. The rest was up front, with no hidden depths. Here nature could not kill human beings as it still did on natural planets.

I turned to face the door and pressed my palm on

the lock. The massive panel slid open and I went inside. As the outer door closed, the inner one slid open. I triggered a long string of lights as I came out into the low-ceilinged corridor.

I walked to the observatory at the end of the passage, where I pressed my palm again and stepped into a large circular chamber covered with screens.

Brain-core terminal work desks stood like mushrooms in the central area. I had helped build parts of the modest observatory. From here, the Sun would be monitored and space scanned for debris and meteors; spacialists would come from all over to study our star. The research station on Mercury was finally being closed down, to the relief of the staff.

I stepped up to the master controls and turned on the three-dee screens. Half were visual displays; the rest revealed the universe in narrow ranges—the radio universe, the neutrino universe, gravitational images of various sectors—all in color enhancements.

The stars turned, circling like some gigantic clockwork around the axis of the rotating hollow.

As I stood there, seemingly at the center of all immensity, I played an old game with myself, the same one I had played as a child—talking to my future self when I felt down, making him promise to remember me, to think back along the time lines of possibility to where I was in bed that night, thinking ahead to him. . . .

And here I was, that future self, thinking back to that

lonely boy who was still with me. Futures cast shadows back into the present. You move ahead as long as you can see the shadows of promises, but when you lose sight of what may be, you bog down in a hopeless present; there is nothing to pull you ahead—the self that looks back is no longer waiting for you up in the future; your future becomes the present, and soon it becomes the past. If I could keep a balance between what I had been, what I was now, and what I might become, then I would be okay for a long time.

I had come to Mercury to gain a sense of doing, of having done something that wasn't only worthy in itself, as Morey was doing, but to see the good of doing it. Morey would see the result of what he was doing later; I hadn't been willing to wait. Maybe one day I would become more patient, more willing to look for hidden values.

I didn't know what lay ahead, and down deep I was glad of it. Life had not closed itself up around me, as it had for so many people of the late twentieth century. I didn't know where home would be, and that seemed best.

Ro found me as I was cycling back in the morning.

"How is my beautiful boy?" she asked, smiling. I kissed her deeply, shivering in the morning chill.

We went into the hills and stayed in the tall grass until we were very tired.

"So you think you've figured me out," I said later. Ro was looking at me knowingly as we relaxed.

"I think so."

"We've had this conversation before, but go ahead, I'm curious."

"You were an overprotected kid. You had it easy, but you left home and found out things were very tough for a lot of people, and you felt guilty. You needed to find out—to test yourself, to do something that would give you a sense of responsibility and control. As an only child you needed other people to draw you out of yourself, and you found them. I know—I wanted the same thing."

"I know all that. What else did we find out?"

"That we can do, and learn, win out over doubts."

"Is that all? I would have thought it would be more." I was being deliberately perverse.

"Well—there was the fear of failure to overcome. . . ."

"What else? Come on."

"Well—you started out wanting to be like Morey but decided to be yourself."

"And is that any good?"

"Different—but just as good."

"And that's what you think of me?"

She laughed. "Don't ask too much. You're just *beginning* to be yourself."

I made a funny face. "How did you find all this out?"

"Oh—Linda told me."

"What?"

"And Bernie, Jake, Morey, you, and everything around you."

"Spy!" I bit her bare stomach—gently, of course.

"By the way," she said after a while, "what *are* we going to do? Do you want to go out to Ceres, or Saturn? We've *got* to make plans."

"What do you think?"

"I like going where new things are being done," she said firmly.

"Same here," I replied.

The Sun lost its watercolor paleness as it brightened toward noon, and we walked back with its warmth on our faces.

21 SUNSPACER

Sometimes I look toward Earth and see myself sitting in my high school cafeteria, gazing out through the three-dee motion mural at the parade of planets, imagining that I'm falling toward Saturn, into the rings of ice and debris—

—and I have to remind myself that I am out here, in the Rings of Saturn, helping to build a cluster of habitats; major centers are growing in orbit around the largest moons, which together with the rings are a plentiful source of raw materials. There are even plans for a tourist hotel.

If the Sun should suddenly expand into a red giant and gobble up the inner worlds of Mercury, Venus, Earth, and Mars, civilization out here would merely be warmed, we're so far away.

Bit by bit, humankind is shaping the resources of Sunspace into places for life. Millions of inner spaces will one day circle the Sun, forming at first a series of spaced rings, and finally a shell of life enclosing the Sun. The planets will be gone by then, used up for raw materials, but the place names and scenic locales will endure inside the habitats.

I have worked my way to the edge of a new life, but I will have to go the rest of the way to see it whole. Mistakes—my own and those of others—wait for me; but there is room for mistakes out here, where they can no longer cost the life of humanity's only home. Frontiers can absorb errors on a grand scale, you see; that was what was wrong with the rise of technical civilization on the surface of Earth. The vulnerability of an overcrowded, overindustrialized natural planet made human failure count for too much in the last century. Out here, we don't have to depend on people being perfect; our industrial and human wastes disappear into an ocean of night that can never be polluted. As it happens, we don't throw much of anything away; most of it goes into our fusion recyclers. Anyway, the point is that humanity is too widespread, too constructive, to ever be in danger of killing itself off again.

"Are you sure you want to go?" I asked Ro at the end of our Mercury contract.

"I want to work in strange places," she said with a straight face.

By the time we left, the habitat was working smoothly. There were a few problems with shielding, and a small fire in one of the hotel rooms gave us a scare on my birthday. The town lights had been a sprinkle of starlight on the lake that night, when a meteor had knocked out the external optics, throwing the hollow into darkness— but the towns simply kept their lights going until the Sun winked on again. Extra shielding on the outside rig was all that had been needed.

But the most important thing happened just as we were leaving. The big robots arrived and were sent down to Mercury. They would do *all* the heavy mining, refining, repairs, and launching of slugs. These were the most advanced machines, a thousand times better than the previous ones. Working through computer links, the miners would program these titans to go anywhere on the planet; human eyes would look over their shoulders, going where no human flesh, or previous robots, could survive. Fewer miners would be needed on the surface as time went on; fewer lives would be risked. I thought of the empty underground towns where we had almost lost our lives. Old Merk would finally get its way, and one day the warrens would be destroyed.

Bob Svoboda became a programmer-operator, working with the robot titans and the Brain-Core intelligences. He married Helen Wodka a year after we left.

We ran into quite a few people from the Mercury project around Saturn, Jake and Linda among them. Both are interested in the same project Ro and I have applied for—as hands on the expedition to Titan's north pole. A large amphibious crawler-submarine will be placed on the surface, if possible, and it will try to reach the pole, by submerging if necessary. The training will be invaluable, and the experience might help us get on one of the big habitat starships now under construction around Titan.

It's awesome here in the Rings. The big planet's beauty creeps up on you, no matter how long you've been here. The planet seems nearby, floating casually, except something that big can't really be casual. In my sleep I sink through its mysterious ocean of gas and liquid, feeling with my feet for a bottom which may or may not be there, thousands of miles below. . . .

A dozen habitats are nearing completion around Titan alone. Ro and I learned today that the Centauri Starship's crew will be chosen from those of us who go on the polar jaunt. It's the only way of having a chance at the starship.

Where is home?

All of Sunspace is home. Those of us who work outside Earth's planetary womb are the eyes, ears, and hands of humanity, reaching out to the stars. Our Sun is only a common star, but the starlight sings eternal across the Milky Way, which is only one of the countless galaxies fleeing toward the edge of space-time. To go out among them, you have to keep changing; you have to burn inside, to hold back the dark; you have to want the vastness that is so full of possibilities, and know that it is a place of infinite beauty in which to test human courage and intelligence; you must feel deep space opening up in your heart, drink the strange light that flows into your eyes from far stars, and love the singing silence in your ears.

You have to care a lot.

ABOUT THE AUTHOR

George Zebrowski is the author of more than forty short stories appearing in magazines and anthologies since 1970. His several novels have been translated into six languages, among them Swedish and Japanese. *The Monadic Universe*, a collection of his stories, appeared in 1977. He has edited anthologies for Harper & Row, Doubleday, and Random House. Crown is the publisher of his most recent anthology, *Creations* (co-edited with Isaac Asimov and Martin Greenberg). *Macrolife*, his most recent novel, was published by Harper & Row and reprinted by Avon. *The Omega Point Trilogy* has just been published by Ace; this is the first one-volume edition, incorporating his first novel from 1972. A book about his work will be published in the near future.

Born in Austria of refugee Poles who were exported to the German Reich as slave labor, he grew up in England and New York City. He is now a full-time writer, with many books planned for publication in the near future.